CALLING HER HOME

S.E. Chandler

Calling Her Home

Visit S.E. Chandler online:

Facebook.com/SEChandlerBooks
SEChandlerBooks.com
Connect@SEChandlerBooks.com

For Mom, my first Super Fan,

Thank you for believing in the best of me all this
time.

S

Table of Contents

Chapter 1

A muffled snap of sheets in the breeze drew my attention. The delicious warmth of satisfaction rippled through my flesh as I recognized that familiar post-orgasm relaxation. Unsure of the billowy sheets indoors, I was alone as my surroundings came into focus: white fabric hanging in layers around this room I didn't know; lying nude in three thousand-something count, super-soft sheets; the glow of early morning pooled in pinkish layers; the earthy smell of an open window in the Spring and remnants of boozy sex.

This was a dream, I realized—a very good dream. I saw an outline of a figure moving through the sheets. I sat up on my elbows and strained to see if it was someone I knew or another stranger. The shifting sheets parted just enough to catch a glimpse from her mid-back to calf. She was a long-haired blonde with smooth back and ass, gliding silently across the floor, the fingers of her left hand flitting along the sheet. I fought the urge to collapse back in the sheets while craving more of whatever had just happened when I saw the modest tattoo on her left shoulder blade—a delicate, opened, white lotus.

As much as I wanted to stay, my senses were overloaded with signals, and I rose sharply from the dream. Maybe if I fell back asleep, I could slip back to the mysterious lotus girl and the sweet possibility of more fabulous fucking.

That only happens when I'm having some horrible dream about trying to get on the subway, but the signs are all blurry and some jackass who just threw ice cream at me is chasing me with an umbrella.

I surrendered and opened my eyes to a lazy Saturday morning I would not spend working. Maru was awake, quite awake, and looking directly at me. I reached for her hip under the sheets and squeezed.

"Everything ok?" I asked, wondering how long she had been watching.

She dashed half a smile but did not reply. She laced her fingers through my hand on her hip, pulled them over the covers and kissed my knuckles. I shifted and snuggled closer thinking she and I could pick up where I left from the dream.

"I just had the wildest dream," I said, tangling my legs between hers. "A sex dream." My voice was far from husky, but the low rasp was about as close as I got to saying "get over here" with a tone.

She rolled out from under me and faked a stretch. Her arms and legs went out stiff, but no tremble for that first-thing-in-the-morning stretch.

"Hey," I said, and propped up an elbow. "Is everything ok?"

"I'm hungry," she said. "What do you want for breakfast?"

"Have you been up for a minute?"

"Just a bit."

"Oh, sorry. I was apparently really enjoying myself." I laughed and tried to bring the conversation back to the task at hand.

"Sounds like it," she said, getting out from under the covers and reaching for a T-shirt. Plain white.

Like always. I apparently really enjoyed myself and even still felt silky wetness between my thighs. I hoped I could still capitalize on the moment and lure her back before she put on that damn T-Shirt. I threw myself over the covers reaching for her hand.

"I can show you," I said, eyebrows up, pulling her down. She sat on the bed next to me and scuffed my forehead with a cursory kiss.

"It's 9:30, Vann. What do you want for breakfast?" Ever the optimist, I tossed my hair out of the way and kissed her bronze upper thigh a few times creeping higher, wider and wetter with every breathy kiss.

"Just you," I said into the crease of her hip.

"Then you're getting whatever I make for breakfast."

"Really? That's it? I'm throwing myself at you here and you're just 'I'm hungry?'"

"I am hungry, V," she frowned.

"Since when have you been too hungry for sex? And since when did you care it was 9:30. On a Saturday?" I sat up, rearranging myself to let it go. "Never mind." I softened my tone and stroked her back. "How about if I make breakfast today?"

"How about we make breakfast together?" She smiled again and pulled me up.

"Sure. Omelets?"

"Egg whites and spinach?" she asked, pulling on that damn T-Shirt.

"And mushrooms and onions," I called to her on the way to the bathroom.

That Saturday, we planned on hitting the gym for a late morning spin class. Afterward we'd take Grover out to the dog park for some quality leg lifting and butt sniffing. He was an eclectic mix of a Carin Terrier, what Maru called a Dorothy dog from the Wizard of Oz, and something with a stub nose and tail. He's not much to look at, but he makes up for it in enthusiasm for being our dog.

On weeknights, I took him to our complex's dog yard no longer than he needed to tucker out before bustling back to the apartment, so we all three looked forward to a longer play date at the bigger park on the weekends. If we had time, we'd stop by Iliad Bookshop, a used bookstore in North Hollywood. I wanted to check out a trade and sale special where I could unload all of my books from the last special for half as many new ones.

Maru would work that night at Hama Sushi, the raw fish diner where we met. Hama was a no-nonsense, shotgun dive in Little Tokyo just across from the Japanese American National Museum which was totally fitting because Maru was first generation Japanese American. Her parents were both from Tokyo but met in the states taking refuge in each other's poor English and home feel.

Known for its hard-core albacore, Hama had a long list of rules: no tempura, no teriyaki, no noodles, no rice, no cell phones, and a minimum charge. I found it's random knick-knacks and outdated décor charming but chose it for the authentic Japanese. If you're willing to wait, the friendly service and full flavor was worth it. The menu was epic, but I was there for the yellow tail, quite ironically it would later prove.

Maru was their senior itamae—a sushi Zen master—and worked the busy weekends. The place closed at 10:00, so I never expected Maru home until 11:30 or midnight after clean up and prep work was done. I was usually already asleep unless I got sucked into some sappy movie or late-night binge watching. If I didn't hear her get in the shower, I always felt her slide into bed and draped myself over her.

Maru would be off to work by 2:00, I would pick up around the house and dive face-first into whatever book I had picked up at Iliad. Charming, right? The lustrous life of an eight-year married couple. Not to be underdone by my super boring job as a programming analyst for Houlihan Lokey, a financial advisory firm. It was never boring to me, but any time someone asked me what I do, and I say, "I analyze computer code," they change the subject to the weather, drinking water or something easy. It paid well but didn't make much for conversation.

It was also highly addictive for the right kind of nerd. In finance, the difference is an edge that keeps slipping and changing. Whenever Maru worked late, I found myself working at home. Maybe I was bored. Maybe I was boring.

Either way, I remember that mundane Saturday not because I ended up getting a sweet trade on a Cara Malone lesfic, romantic suspense novel at the Iliad. But because the proverbial rug was about to be ripped from under me that night, then thrown out the window, beaten and burned until my life was no longer recognizable as that ordinary routine I failed to appreciate at 9:30 that morning. Because of the panic that would ensue after Maru's shift at Hama, I was about to become someone else entirely.

Chapter 2

Around 11:30, I nodded off between lines of Radio Silence. I'd been planning to read until Maru got home, maybe shower with her and maybe more. I was done for sure. Our Siamese, Emi, which means something like pretty or sweet or pretty sweet in Japanese, was purring like a lumberjack beside me in bed. I checked the window for familiar lights on the street one more time, clicked off the glow of the moon lamp and was gone after a few breaths.

Maybe I snorted myself awake; maybe Grover licked himself until it woke me up—whatever, I came to through gauzy haze of sleep and realized I was alone. Not sure if I'd been asleep for two minutes or two hours, I reached for my phone to check the time. The light from my iPhone filled the room with a bluish glow. 3:18 a.m. read the huge letters. 3:18 a.m.? I checked again. A rush of panic swelled over me and surged energy to my fuzzy focus. Adrenaline burned off any haziness, and I was up and moving in jerky twitches.

I turned the phone around and used it like a flashlight looking for her clothes, her shoulder bag, thinking maybe she had sacked out on the couch. She did that sometimes if it was a late night. Skip the shower and collapse on the couch. But no, nothing moved, no wallet on the dresser, no keys. Grover raised his head to check out the flurry of activity and sprang to his feet, tail wagging.

"Maru?" I called crossing into the living room as I headed for the bathroom. I checked my phone for messages while I peed at Olympic speed. No text, no missed call, Messager, no email, no nada. I pulled on boxer shorts and a tank top and moved through the living room to the office. The office was really a second bedroom, our luxury. Since we had two incomes and no kids, we paid up for the extra space for me to work from home and for Maru to have a place to work on her characters. Her characters—right, maybe she was back there working on her precious lost language. Not to be ugly, but seriously, the language wasn't lost—just not as regularly employed as past millennia.

Maru's hobby was complicated and confusing. And it was also beautiful. Not everyone knew how to ingest it, but it was unique, and I loved it. She would write traditional Japanese haiku (nature themes, 5, 7, 5 metered lines), then couple it with Tibetan Buddhist characters that amplified, accented or confounded the poem in some way. She used the 9th century Tibetan characters originally used to translate Buddhist scriptures. She explained all this to me, more than once, but I'm sure I didn't catch the significance of a Japanese Zen Buddhist Lesbian colliding conventional haiku with ancient characters of a different tradition, language, and lineage. But just the thought that she might be back in the office painting the decorative symbols over three lines of mysterious text brought immediate relief.

Until I opened the door to the office. Besides Grover, Emi and me, our apartment was empty. I sucked in a jagged shaft of air, steadied myself in the doorway of the office and tried to calm down.

This was going to be one of those times I got all worried and find out she went out with the Hama crew after her shift and then get really mad while she professes to have not realized how late it was or to have forgotten to call or was just about to call or...maybe she was robbed at knife point, in a car wreck or worse.

I barked Siri to call Mary—she never understood Maru, not once. I eventually changed her name in my phone to Mary to get the damn racist to call my wife—when I saw the blinking light on the home phone. We may have been the last home in LA to have a home phone, but I used it for a work fax and our alarm system.

Had I missed a call? My cell rang in one ear when I pushed play on the home phone.

"You have one new message," the voicemail man screeched from the speaker.

I know! Play it! I pressed play again, the phone on its third or fourth ring.

"Message received...today...at 8:50 p.m....." Must have missed the call during Grover's last trip outside before I got ready for bed. He danced in circles at my feet because it didn't matter what time it is. The first one up took him outside.

"Just a minute, buddy," I said, pressing play on the machine.

"Hey Vann, it's me," my friend Kate's voice burst from the machine, the volume much louder than Mr. Voicemail Man. Maru's voicemail picked up at the same time.

"Konnichiwa! This is Maru Wakahisa."

"Just calling to confirm our dinner date for tomorrow night since I never heard back from you and can't get you on your cell..." Discombobulated by the messages playing over one another, I hit stop on the voicemail and waited for Maru's voicemail to start recording.

"Message deleted." Mr. Voicemail Man said too cheery, which wasn't too cheery if it were a telemarketer. I was sure he knew I meant to stop the message, not delete and was just gloating. Damn! I made a mental note to cancel my home phone and see how far I could throw the wireless receiver.

"Hey, it's me. Where are you? It's 3:30 and I'm trying not to worry, but I'm freaking out. Call me as soon as you get this. I'm seriously freaking out."

I touched "End" on the phone and pressed play on the answering machine.

"You have no new messages," he said. Damn. I sort of remembered my date with Kate. Sorting that out would have to wait.

I eye-balled my keys on the table by the front door.

"Calm down, Vann." I told myself. "She's fine, it's nothing—just find her."

I didn't feel fine, I couldn't even feel the essence of fineness in the thick folds of panic. Where was she? I toggled over to text her.

Where are you???? Call me!!!

Excessive punctuation was inexcusable, but I couldn't see myself punching in some non-terrified form of communication at that point. I had no messages, none, no indication from her at all. It was just bizarre; also rude, but way out of character for her.

I pulled up the Find My iPhone app and bit my lip as I waited for satellites to tilt toward her phone and tell me where the fuck she was. As soon as all the devices were loaded, I touched "Mary," because of racist Siri who only speaks Yankee English. The map populated at its extensive leisure and pinpointed Maru's phone as being...still at Hama Sushi. Ok, maybe they were slammed, and I was really paranoid. I toggled back to my contacts and pulled up "Mary Work".

It rang twice before an answering machine picked up and told me they were closed, and they're regular hours were...I ended the call and touched the number again. Maybe they couldn't get to the phone before the machine picked up. Two more rings then the answering machine again. I tried a third time, same result.

"Damn!" I yelled out loud and kicked the kitchen cabinet. Grover skittered away.

"I'm sorry, buddy," I said, going over to comfort him. He immediately put his ears up, ready to go outside again, all forgiven. I grabbed his leash by the door and wrangled him to clip in the latch. I barely snatched the phone from the counter as he dragged me in a beeline for the "Pet Relief Station" in the courtyard behind our apartment.

While he sniffed everything, I thumbed through my contacts looking for a coworker of Maru's that we had hung out with a couple times. I didn't remember his name—something Japanese—so I thought it wouldn't be too hard to find. Scrolling, scrolling, stumbling along behind Grover until the leash went slack. He could have peed on me and I'm not sure I would have noticed.

Karl, Kate, Kathy, Katsu! That had to be it. I paused briefly before touching the number and calling this guy I barely knew at 3:30 in the morning. Grover jerked at the end of the leash and my thumb bumped the number anyway. It started ringing and I pulled back on Grover while I waited for the voice on the other end.

"Hello?" a gruff voice crackled in my ear. Not what I was expecting.

"Katsu? Is that you?"

"Who is this?" He sounded annoyed—and asleep.

"It's Vann."

"Who?"

"Vann Townsend." I tried not to whine. "Maru's wife."

"Maru? Oh, ok. What time is it?"

"It's early, I'm sorry. I just thought—"

"It's 3:30, Vann!" He had just checked the time. "Why are you calling me at fucking 3:30?"

"I realize it's fucking 3:30, Katsu." I sounded like a real bitch. "I'm looking for Maru and thought she might be with you."

"Why would she be with me at 3:30 in the morning?" I could tell by his tone he was really saying 'She's not into guys, so there's no reason she would be with him at that hour.' Or maybe insinuating that I was stupid for asking.

"Because you work together." I retaliated with a snide tone, which thinking about it now was probably an honest question. But I was in full-on freak-out, and this was not the time for political correctness or accurate interpretation of the testosterone/estrogen communication lapse. "I thought you might be staying out for drinks or something."

"Jesus, Vann. I can't even sort out what you're talking about. We had a really crazy night, stayed until like 11:30, I don't know." I heard him swallow a drink of something. "Or was that last night?"

"Did you work with her tonight or not, Katsu? I'm freaking out here!"

"Hey, you're the one who called me while I was asleep after working all damn night asking all this crazy shit."

"So, you worked tonight."

"Yes, yes I worked."

"Was she there?"

"Maru? Yeah, she..." He trailed off.

"She what?"

"What's going on with you two?"

"That's what I'm trying to find out, Katsu!" I exploded. "She hasn't come home; her phone says she's still at work. Did she tell you something?"

"No, nothing like that."

"Then like what?"

"What do you mean, 'like what'?" He amplified his annoyance here.

"Was there something wrong or out of the ordinary, anything?"

"No, man. She just came in, we did our thing and left."

"But she didn't leave, Katsu." I whined. This guy needed some Psychic Friends Network lessons because I was about to come through the phone and strangle him. He clearly did not speak Womanese.

"Well, I guess not."

"Really?" I groaned into the phone.

"We went out to our cars; I got in and drove away. I guess she was still there."

"When, Kat?"

"I told you. Like 11:30." Something like a flood broke open in my chest. Anger, frustration and confusion collided with helplessness and powerlessness.

"Look, I'm sorry. I'm really worried. I can't get her on the phone, nothing." I started crying and heaved ugly and uncontrollable. Grover jumped his front feet up on my right thigh to comfort me smearing mud and whatever else from the dog yard. "I'm freaking out and I have no idea what to do."

"Hey, hey. It's ok, Vann. It's probably nothing, really. Just calm down."

"I'm sorry I was a shit to you. I don't know what I was thinking." I started coming apart. My semblance of a plan overtaken by fear, any focus I had was spread wide by panic. I staggered back to the apartment, completely forgetting about Grover who was a good boy to follow behind me even though it was just for the treat he usually gets for going outside.

"Do you want me to go up to Hama?"

"Oh, that's a good idea." I said, focus returning.

"I can put on some pants—"

"No, no. I'll go up there. I'm up. I'll just check and make sure everything's ok."

"Are you sure?"

"Yes, thank you for not hanging up on me. I know I'm crazy right now."

"I'm sure I would be too. This will all be funny in the morning, right?"

"It better be." I tried to laugh and sobered up a bit. "Thanks, Katsu."

"Ok, call me back if something happens." His tone was soft and sweet. Men will do anything to quell a crying woman, but I refused to take advantage of him.

"I will. Thanks again."

I clasped on a bra under my tank top and pulled a pair of cargo shorts over the boxers. Slipping into some flip flops by the door, I grabbed the keys and a hat and headed for my silver Volkswagen Jetta. It chirped twice and flashed the lights across the parking lot as I unlocked the driver's door. I jumped in, cranked the engine and threw it into reverse, and headed toward the sushi shop punching Maru's cell one more time.

* * *

On the drive toward the pulsing signal of Maru's phone, my thoughts oscillated between being scared—truly fearful for her life—and an unadulterated rage that I visualized as slapping the shit out of her when I saw her. I thought if she was dead in the alley, I would probably slap the shit out of her anyway. Really, I wouldn't. But I was so pissed that she made me worried. I was mad at myself for worrying, for letting myself love someone so much that I would drive around at 4:00 in the morning looking for her.

Honestly, she made me crazy. I had become an insane person in our eight years together. She was this golden honey thing I wanted to keep forever. Past boyfriends weren't like that. If they didn't show up at 3:30 in the morning, I was like, 'whatever—move on'. Thinking he cheated or wasn't that good anyway, but not Maru. She put me first, always giving of herself. She was need; she was home; she was making me a fanatical, love-sick idiot. And now she was missing, and I was coming apart like that sweater in that Weezer song. It sounded stupid but was so true.

As I moved forward in the blindness of that night, my sweater of safety was becoming completely unraveled. I couldn't control or calm myself—a mop bucket dumped over on the floor that just keeps spreading and spreading and no number of towels would soak it up. My thoughts poured out and over each other: terrible, sad, angry, projections of all kinds, until I was pulling into the dark lot behind Hama Sushi right next to Maru's Mitsubishi Eclipse.

Relief. Quickly whooshed aside by vehement fury. The white-hot, killer kind. How could she have done this? Just not call. I threw open my car door and marched around to her driver-side window. I pounded with my fist before I realized she wasn't inside.

She wasn't in the car. I paused to process and quickly directed my wrath toward the backdoor of Hama. An overhead light was on near the dumpster by the building, but it was otherwise dark. I banged on the back door and yelled her name. No one came; I pounded again. Still no one. I went to one of the windows and cupped my hands around the sides of my face to look inside. It was totally dark. Not even a light on at the bar.

A huge rush of tingling needles came over me. It started in my hairline and trickled all the way down through my toes, like when your arm falls asleep and starts waking up. I was waking up all right. I tasted something metallic in my mouth, hands shaking. Adrenaline had opened wide and dumped hormones into my system alerting that something was very wrong. I had no idea what I was going to fight or flee from, but I was ready to sprint into the night screaming her name.

When I tried the handle, her car was unlocked. My heart seized again. It felt like someone reached in my chest and squeezed hard. Her phone was in the cup holder, my string of calls and texts unseen. Seeing her wallet in the passenger seat made my knees buckle. I folded into the door facing the back seat, half on the running board, half on the seat. There was no flood of adrenaline this time, just a stab of nausea as the world tilted and faded gray at the edges. I steeled myself in the car door, determined not to pass out or puke. The sweater had unraveled, and this was me, naked.

Chapter 3

I sat in my car outside the Central Community L. A. police department just a few blocks from Hama, from her empty car and scary stuff left behind. I checked myself in the mirror. It was useless. The blotchy redness has set in around my eyes and my nose was already raw from the McDonald's napkins.

I dragged myself up the steps and pulled on the glass door that felt like a thousand pounds to my wasted energy stores. I dug through my purse for ID when I made it to the counter and leaned heavily into it.

"May I help you?" An overweight officer named Munez looked at me over his reading glasses, no shred of concern on his face. I shriveled a little feeling like I had interrupted an important crossword puzzle.

"Yes, I need to file..." I took a deep breath in the levity of reality. "a missing person's report." The words shot out of my mouth like a pinched hose being released, I may have spit on Munez. Tears started up and whatever composure I had gathered in the parking lot fell apart.

"How long has the person been missing?" he asked flatly.

"What? I'm not sure; I just need to—"

"How long has the person been missing, ma'am? I have to know for the report."

"I don't know, Officer. She was supposed to be around midnight and never—"

"So less than 24 hours, then?"

"Yes, but—"

"The person must be missing for more than 24 hours before we can file a report, ma'am. Come after it's been at least that long."

"What? No, I need to—"

"You need to come back after it's been at least 24 hours ma'am," he said, dripping with contempt. The fear and fatigue I felt balled up into fury. My fist clenched on the counter in front of him.

"If you would stop interrupting me and let me explain—"

"There's nothing to explain other than we can't do anything until the person has been missing for twenty-four hours." He crossed his arms and leaned back. I was seized with an intense need to pick up the receiver of his phone and beat him severely. I closed my eyes and tried to remember where I was before I assaulted an officer.

"Ok. I'm clearly not getting anywhere with you and it's making me very upset. I need to speak to someone else."

"I'm sure you upset; everyone is." He smiled at me.

"Listen, Officer Munez," I said, making a horrible decision to thump his name plate. "My wife is missing. She didn't come home; her car was abandoned at her work with her phone, keys and wallet still in it. So, there is clearly something very wrong here. And you're going to help me or find someone who will." He looked down at the flicked name plate and slowly brought his gaze up to mine. Flames shot from them burning a hole in my face.

He folded his fingers in front of him and leaned forward. "You listen." His lower lip glistened. "When your wife..." he used air quotes and spit out the "f." "Has been missing for 24 hours, come back.

Unless you have other business here, I suggest you leave immediately." In no mood to back down or go to jail, I wouldn't slink away and let the bastard win.

"So that's it. That's all you do?" I stared him down, but he gave no sign of changing his mind, just that glare. "Someone is in real trouble here. I-I have evidence and you're just going to sit there and go back to your crossword puzzle?"

He smirked. He knew I goaded him, but I'm sure he'd been trained not to give into the whims of whiners, crying woman or not. This man had no soul. "Unless you have some other business here, ma'am, I suggest you leave."

"Way to protect and serve, there, Munez," I said. I hauled my purse over my shoulder and banged my keys against the counter. I hoped to create a scene so everyone would see what a dick this guy was to poor little me. But there wasn't anyone around and it probably didn't matter.

"If something has happened to her, that's on you." I said trembling. A couple of tears slipped out. "That's on you." I pushed away from the counter and stomped across the station to the exit. I looked back at him with my most pathetic face at the door, but he stared at me pushing me out with his glare. It was chilling and nauseating at the same time.

In my car, I gripped the wheel with both hands and sobbed hysterical, jagged heaves of moans and gasps. It was ugly. I never cried pretty anyway, but this was desperate retching. I had no idea what to do. She's gone I repeated over and over. I didn't know where to look. Where would she be without her car, her phone, her money? Nowhere good. My mind was cruel. Gruesome scenes of her beautiful body twisted and bleeding somewhere flashed on a loop. Who would do something to her?

I couldn't sort through the images and emotions to formulate any actual action. I just sat there in the parking lot bawling. How was I supposed to get someone to help me? How could I get the police to look for her?

An idea shot through the thicket of horror that seemed viable. I would go back to Hama and ram my car into hers, call and report and accident and cops would have to come. Then someone would listen to me. That was a great idea, I thought! It was terrible and not completely thought through but seemed reasonable at the time. I sucked up a few heaves and wiped my nose with the last usable corner of my napkin before turning the key. I put the car in reverse and looked over my shoulder, ready to head back to Hama Sushi and total both our cars.

Bang! Bang! Bang! The hard metallic sound burst from my driver side window, sending a jolt through me. I mashed the gas pedal. The car jolted back a few yards before I braked and looked over. Someone was shined a flashlight in my windshield and yelled from next to where I was parked. I rolled down my window and shielded my eyes.

"I'm sorry, ma'am. I didn't mean to scare you, there." It was a woman's voice and by the position of the flashlight by the shoulder, a cop. She lowered the light, and I could see I was right.

"Have I done something wrong, officer?" I asked, voice still wobbly.

"You want to pull out of the street ma'am?" She flagged me to park as she headed over to my open window. She put her hands on her knees to lower to my window height.

"Did I do something wrong?"

"No ma'am. I don't want you to get hit in the street." Not that it was going to matter since I was about to run my car into Maru's, I thought. The absurdity of my plan seeped in through my desperation. I pulled back into the spot and put it in park.

"Thanks." She chuckled. She was different from Officer Asshole I had just encountered: concerned, compassionate and going out of her way to help me.

"I'm Officer White." She looked back over her shoulder at the police station.

"I'm Vann. Vann Townsend." I stuck my hand out and she shook it warmly.

"Hey, listen, I heard what happened with Munez."

"You did?"

"Yeah, I'm sorry about that. He's a real stickler for...policy."

"Is it against policy to report someone missing?"

"No ma'am. But you do have to wait 24 hours before we can file a report." I bit my lip and nodded wondering why she followed me all the way out here to remind me of what her colleague had explained four times.

"Ok, so....?" I asked. She checked the front door again.

"Well, if you think there's been a crime, I can take your statement."

"Really?" I asked hopefully. "Why didn't he just say that? I have a statement; I mean I can give a statement."

"Munez? Well, let's just say I'd be more sympathetic to your...situation," she got out the word but lowered her voice. "And I'd like to help you out if I can."

"My situation?" I said imitating her tone. "You can help me?"

"I'm not sure, but I can take your statement."

"Oh! My situation. You mean my wife?" She checked the door again.

"Well, yes. Just get some information."

"I don't understand, Officer. Marriage is legal here and you seem very nervous like you'll get in trouble for talking to me. If there was something that could be done, why would it matter who I was married to?" It was too much. I was preaching to the choir but was still disdainful.

"Yes, ma'am. You're right," she said and looked at the door but didn't turn back to me. "Tolerance is not acceptance, though."

"I'm sorry, Officer. That was rude. You're clearly trying to help me. I'm just a wreck right now."

"It's alright; I would be too. Would you like to come back inside and make a statement?"

"Is it OK? Will you get in trouble?"

"It'll be fine. I have an office we can use—for confidentiality. You know."

"Yes, thank you so much. I mean really." I said getting out of my car. "You didn't have to do this, and I appreciate you trying to do something."

"Protect and serve, right?" she joked. I nodded and had to laugh too, then followed her back inside.

Munez was away from the desk when we passed by and I thought 'how convenient,' and wished I could have made a nasty face at him. Officer White was a lieutenant according to the placard on her desk. I realized she wasn't checking the door to see if she would get in trouble, but to see if she could protect me, probably having told Munez to get lost for a few minutes.

"Lieutenant Jessica White?" I asked with impression in my tone. She smiled while rifling through her desk and produced a writing pad.

"Jess is fine."

"I'm guessing you don't take a lot of statements?"

"No, not much anymore."

In the light of her office, I got a better view of her. It was impossible to get an idea of her figure other than 'fit' under her uniform. But her narrow face was wise and kind, maybe early forties with dishwater blonde hair pulled in a twist.

"Thank you for doing this. Even if it doesn't help, it makes me feel better, like I'm doing something to find her."

"What's her name?"

We went through the whole thing. She scribbled notes, asked questions, asked if there was any chance there was anyone else. I said no, but it hadn't occurred to me to wonder about that. It couldn't be; I would have seen signs, My mind drifted down that nasty path while I answered her other questions. It gnawed at me when we shook hands in the doorway after the interview an hour later. I headed back to my car and pulled up Kate's number on my phone. Six AM wouldn't be too early to call a best friend on a Sunday when your whole world is engulfed in flames.

Chapter 4

Kate Samson was already on her way to my condo before I asked. She was one of those friends, the kind that are better to you than you are to yourself. In the miniscule world of female programmers, we started our careers at Houlihan at the same time. I sat in orientation completely detached from the paperwork and formalities thinking, oh goody—another girl! Then immediately, I hope she's not creepy or weird. As if that wasn't creepy or weird.

Kate was weird in a lovable way. She frequently said the wrong thing, oblivious, but hilarious. To me at least. She once offered to show our supervisor, Mike, how to run spell check on his memos. Funny because she was being helpful, not hateful.

Because I appreciate humor in nearly every form, and she was the only other female on my floor, we became butthole buddies our first week at Houlihan. Our standing date on for drinks on Thursday nights was at the Pink Taco, close enough to knee-walk back to our office after over-indulging in $5 margaritas or sangrias during happy hour. We spent too many hours ragging about work, love and life until way too late for a school night, had to leave our cars in the parking deck and call a cab to get home. Which led to another cab ride back to work in the morning coupled with a hangover and hearty desire to accomplish nothing that had to do with lines of code.

Kate was my BFF, "bestie", whatever. She wouldn't sugar coat my shit show or ooze an apology that didn't help me get my head on straight. She was a problem solver and I need her brain because mine had left the building.

Kate made coffee as soon as she hit the door. She would hand me a tissue before giving me a hug—it's more practical when someone's upset. I filled her in between relentless sobs on the phone. She stopped me and said to wait until she could get here.

"This coffee is just terrible, Vann." She inspected the knock-off bag of Sumatra beans. "Here, drink this." She handed me a cup. I recoiled at the idea of her making me drink something she thought was terrible but took it automatically.

"Thanks," I said, my voice trashed. The treachery of the night had fully set in, and I was a complete wreck. "Thanks for coming."

"Ok, so from what I understand, your woman didn't come home, her coworker didn't know where she was, her car and personal effects are still at work, you couldn't file a police report, but some Lesbo cop took your statement?"

"I didn't say she was a Lesbo. But yes, that's correct."

"Did you get the stuff out of her car?"

"No, I didn't want to move anything."

"Did you at least lock her car when you left it?"

"I don't remember."

"You don't remember if you locked the car?

"No, I don't," I said, and twisted my face like she was supposed to know I couldn't be expected to know such an outlandish thing.

"Let's start with what we do know. When is the 24 hours up?"

"I don't know that either. Does it start from when she was supposed to be home or from when I figured out she wasn't home, or from when her shift ended and Katsu saw her last?"

"Do you think we could get away with starting when she left for work? I mean, how will they know Katsu saw her when they were leaving around 11:30."

"Probably because I told Jess he told me she was there."

"Jess?"

"The Lesbo officer."

"You call her by her first name?"

"She asked me to."

"Kinky, but ok. There goes that idea. Looks like we'll have to wait until 11:30 tonight to file the formal missing person's report."

"I don't think I can wait that long. I'm totally blitzed; freaking out here."

"What can we do about this 'statement' your girlfriend, Jess, took?"

"Don't say it rude like that. She was trying to help me."

"I'm sure she was," she smirked.

"Fuck you. I'm married—"

"Not sorry. Ok, focus. The statement?"

"I don't know. I mean, I thought about ramming my car into hers so police would have to come and start an investigation."

"That was your brilliant idea?"

"I didn't know else to do. That asshole had just thrown me out on my ear, and I was in a total panic."

"Don't say things like that; it makes you sound old."

"Like what?"

"Thrown out on your ear."

"Who are you to tell me what to say, Miss Awkward Conversation. And why do I even care if I sound old? I am old!"

"You're 29, V. Just trust me here."

"That's still older than you."

"True, but focus. Obviously wrecking both your cars is a bad idea. What about the statement?"

"I don't know. I think she was just trying to help."

"Really helpful, V. Maybe she was trying to help herself."

"Hey!" I slapped her arm.

"Ok, sorry for that one. So, what are the most likely scenarios here?"

"She was kidnapped."

"Who would want to kidnap her and why? Even if they wanted money, they would have taken her wallet or something. Has anyone called you about a kidnapping?"

"No, smart ass."

"I'm not being a smart ass. I'm just thinking out loud."

"Your out loud thinker is a smart ass."

"What does that even mean?"

"What if she was taken at gunpoint and raped or something. Oh god," I dropped my face into my hands shaking my head.

"Uh, not likely. Isn't Maru some Judo master?"

"No, aikido. Not the same thing."

"But if someone tried to attack her, she would be able to jack them up, right?"

"More like make them fall down."

"Work with me here, Vann. She can defend herself and is very strong, yes?"

"Yes."

"Ok, so what else?"

"I don't know, Kate. Why does someone just go missing?"

"Oh, I don't know, V." Her tone dripped with sarcasm. "Did she owe someone money?" She took a drink from her coffee cup and made a disgusted face.

"That's silly."

"Is it? Maybe she had a gambling problem."

"Don't you think I would notice something stupid like that."

"Ok, then was she fucking someone else." Kate dropped her hands, resolute.

"No!" I was reviled and shot up from my stool at the counter. "How could you even think that?"

"Because it happens to oh, 60 percent of couples out there." She shrugged.

"Not us. You don't spend eight years with someone and not know there's something wrong like that. I know her, all of her."

"Do you?"

"Yes, dammit. And that doesn't make any sense anyway? Why would she leave her fucking car and keys and shit if she was just running off with someone else, Kate."

"I'm trying to be realistic here. We've got to look at everything, right?"

"Not that. Not that."

"Are you sure everything was alright? I mean, do you remember any strange behavior from her recently?"

"No, Kate. I'm telling you, we are fine. And stop talking in past tense; it makes me nervous." Just then, a memory shot to the surface of my haze that stilled me abruptly. I didn't think anything about it at the time, but it was like a cold slap now: Maru's face, her eyes locked on mine, blankly looking through me.

"What?" Kate had noticed. I did not want to pursue this avenue.

"Nothing." My eyes shifted up to the right, an obvious tell that I was in memory.

"No, not nothing. What is it?"

"Yesterday morning..." I stopped trying to piece it together and find some clues I could explain away before divulging to her.

"What happened the morning your wife disappeared, Vann?" I locked eyes with her, pled not to have to say it out loud, like it would fundamentally change me. I was throttled by stupid fears that fall all around you in times of extreme distress and disorientation. "You need me to ask these tough questions." She pressed.

"I was waking up from this...dream."

"Why do you say it like that? Dream?"

"It was this really hot, sex dream, and I was feeling kind of...you know."

"Yeah, I think I do. So what?"

"Well, when I woke up, Maru was already awake and looking right at me, right through me really."

"Does that mean anything to you?"

"No, nothing. I didn't even think anything about it until just now when you asked if she was acting funny or whatever. It's the first time I remember her turning down sex, too." Kate narrowed her eyes and pursed her lips in a deep-thinking gesture.

She launched herself from the edge of the counter leaving her coffee behind and headed for our bedroom. Grover trotted in behind her like they were on the same page.

"Hey, what? What?" I followed them.

"Did she take anything? Clothes, photos, personal items?" She pulled out drawers and skimmed through them.

"Kate, she left her car, wallet and phone," I said. "Don't you think if she was leaving, she might take those personal items?"

"Maybe."

"Maybe? This is stupid."

"Is there something very personal to her that she wouldn't go anywhere without?"

"Really, Kate? I don't know how this is helping."

"A ring, a necklace?"

"She always wore that silver necklace; she had it on when she left. She didn't wear our rings to work."

"Are they here?"

"Yes, they're here."

"That wouldn't make sense anyway."

"That's what I'm trying to tell you." I closed the drawers in front of her before she got to the "unmentionables" that you don't share with friends, unless it's with benefits.

"So, what else could it be?"

"I don't know why you have to jump cheating and leaving."

"I don't know why you have to jump to rape and murder."

"Fair. Is there anything in between?" We were silent, suspended in action.

"What about her family?" Kate asked, a thought had struck her.

"We don't really talk to her family. They're Japanese."

"No really, I couldn't tell because Maru looks Irish."

"Quit being a smartass."

"Quit being a dumbass. Have you heard from them or what?"

"No. I said we don't talk to them. Queers are major faux pas in Japan."

"Oh, and it's widely accepted right here in the old U S of A."

"It's different. You just don't talk about it in their culture."

"So how does that translate to not talking to them at all?"

"It's totally different; you don't understand anything about them."

"And you do?"

"Not exactly but it's something like this. Maru never came out to them. I'm sure they knew. I mean, how can you not know?"

"Short hair, no husband, man's job, 4 percent body fat. Don't tell me you're being stereotypical about your own wife, V." I scowled at her sarcasm.

"Anyway. From what I understand about Japanese culture is that they ostracize you as your punishment."

"How is that punishment? I mean, have you met my family?" She joked.

"It's not funny. They're all about conformity and being a part of a group. They considering ignoring a kid in school bullying. Some kids who were left out have killed themselves."

"Are you serious? That's so sad."

"I know. It's a big deal to not be a part of the group, especially your own family."

"Did her family banish her or something?"

"From what Ru told me, when she left home for college, she never went back."

"Isn't that ideal, though. I mean, only lazy bums go back home after college."

"No, she never went home again. Not for a birthday or a holiday or a death in the family or anything. She never got a call from her folks, and she never made one either."

"That's kind of fucked up, V."

"I know. I talk to my mom and little sister sometimes, go see them every once in a while, so neither of us are really close to our family. We have good friends for family." I smiled at her and squeezed her hand. Some tears came up, but I shooed them away with an upward glance.

"Well, along those lines. Could she have tried to reconnect with them, and they be like, 'sure, you can come back to family land if you lose that Lesbian lover'?"

"I doubt it. She stayed loosely connected to her brother, Daisuke."

"How so?"

"Facebook friends, mostly."

"Oh, that's cold."

"It was what she had. I think they got together maybe once a year or so."

"What's he do?"

"Hell, I don't know. I barely know anything about him other than his name."

"And that he has a Facebook page."

"Yes, and that he's younger than she is."

"So maybe he's cool with the whole 'gay' thing."

"I don't know. I never met him, talked to him, anything."

"Well so what? The question is, would Maru have talked to him?" I crossed my arms, thinking.

"Don't know. Hell, maybe. I just don't know."

"Let's find out," she said, her eyes bright, working her magic.

If I could have paused there for a moment, held time still, I might still be the same person today that I was right then. I was happy being oblivious. I had this quaint little life and cutesy belief that most things work out well. This was the point of no return where, for the first time, I didn't want to know. Didn't want to know what happened, why whatever was going on. I just wanted her back; wanted her to walk through the door like nothing ever happened. Alien abduction, temporary amnesia, whatever, she was just back. Her sweet, salty smell, her arms tangled around my waist, her mouth on my ear and neck, her voice, low, warm and comforting—home. She was my home. Whatever we were about to find out was going to hurt. I knew it in my bones, an ugly threshold I did not want to cross, knowing I could never be that unwounded, carefree girl again. Jaded, party of one, now seating...

Chapter 5

Kate looked over my shoulder at my laptop from beside the couch. I pulled up Facebook and resisted the temptation to check my notifications (there were 6) to see who had 'liked' what or commented on one of my posts or invited me one more time to play Candy Crush. I glanced at my active friends and didn't see the green dot next to Maru's profile letting me know she was online. I went to the search field and keyed in "Ma" to jettison to her page.

No new posts since last night. In fact, no posts since last week. It wasn't unusual. Maru had a quaint list of 75 friends, and mostly commented about or shared other people's posts. Japanese modesty, I always assumed. Sometimes she would post a photo of Evi and/or Grover or repost a quote from the Dalai Lama's FB page she found particularly meaningful. Occasionally she'd put up a photo of some spectacular sushi dish she'd created that looked to be created by a god and left me wishing she'd brought it home for me to fully appreciate and devour.

A private person, she rarely mentioned herself, me or us in her posts. The uber-rare post of a haiku she had written was about as personal as it got. Much unlike the rest of the world that posts incessantly about themselves, their children, where they've been, what they've eaten, anything to impress. Check in at the theatre, check in at a restaurant, check in at check in for a hotel—it was relentless. And of course, being the longtime techie I was, I employed it fully and shamelessly.

I scrolled down to her friends and found Daisuke in the second row. I clicked on his profile photo showing him heavily bundled from the shoulders up: coat, scarf, knit cap; slight smile taken under a streetlight, it looked like. I wondered where he was when he had taken the selfie, and what it meant to him. I clicked on "+1 Add Friend."

"You don't want to add him as a friend, Vann; you want to send him a message." Kate poked the screen above the "Message" button.

"I know, but it can't hurt."

"What, are you going to wait for him to accept your request?"

"No, Kate. I just added him as a friend is all." I was annoyed by her backseat driving.

"We're on the clock here, V."

"Calm yourself. It's taken more time for you to bitch at me about it than to just do it."

"So just message him, already." I had already clicked on "About" which was even sparser than Maru's own page. Hometown: Tokyo. Current City: Los Angeles. Work and Education: student at UCLA Medical School. Looks like somebody was living up to Wakahisa first-generation American standards.

"Seriously? Is this a recon mission or are you just going to message him?" Kate was impatient.

"Looks like he's in medical school. I guess that's what he does for a living."

"No shit. Are you stalling or stalking? What's with you?" I looked up at her with genuine confusion, like 'what do you expect'. Damn right I was delaying this. "Do you want me to steer?" She was referring to taking over the keyboard which we frequently did to each other at work when working through a problem.

"No, I don't want you to steer. I can do this. I can," I said reassuring myself. She must have picked up on the pheromones of fear emanating from me because it I felt her shift and soften.

"Just message him. It'll be ok." I pushed my finger over the sensor pad to the "Message" button and double-tapped. A new message box pulled up, blank and gaping. The cursor blinked, steady, persistent, bossy. "Type, bitch!" it was saying.

"What do I say? I mean how do I say 'Hey, this is your sister's Lesbian lover. Seen her around? I seem to have misplaced her'?"

"Yeah, kind of like that, but I would leave out the 'misplaced' part. It doesn't seem urgent enough," she said matter-of-factly.

"Oh, you have to be kidding me, Kate. I wasn't serious about that."

"How about if you just start with who you are. Just start somewhere."

Just start somewhere. It hung out there like a slow-motion slam-dunk. Waiting for the explosion of action.

"Dear Daisuke, this is Vann Townsend."

I began typing.

"Don't use, 'dear,' it's too formal. Just talk to him," Kate said. I deleted the line of text and started again.

"Good afternoon, Daisuke"

"That's the same thing. Too formal. This is Facebook, not a letter to Congress. Just tell him you're looking for his sister..."

"Oh! I got it!" I started typing in programming speed.

"Konnichiwa! That's what Maru always says anyway. I know this may seem awkward, but I need to talk with you urgently."

"That's better," she encouraged.

"If your sister has shared as little about you with me, I'm sure she's shared the same about me with you. Please know that I love her very much and am only contacting you because I'm concerned about her safety right now."

"Do you think that's too much?" I asked. "I don't want to freak him out."

"No, it conveys urgency plus the who and what without too much detail. Do you want him to call you or meet you or what?"

"I don't know; I hadn't thought about it."

"Let him decide. Just give him some options."

"I don't know how else to contact you and was hoping you would call me so we can talk or meet in person this afternoon. Please contact me AS SOON AS you get this message. I'll be waiting, literally by the phone, for your call."

"Too desperate?" I asked.

"A little; just go with it." I typed in my cell phone number and pressed "Enter" to send the message. It ballooned up in the dialogue box and sat there under the time stamp bar:

--- May 16th, 8:08 a.m. ---

"Well, that's it, I guess," I said looking up at Kate.

"Now we wait."

"I don't think I can."

"What choice do you have?" My eyes fell back down to the glowing computer screen.

"I can choose that bottle of Robert Mondovi on the fridge." Kate plopped down on the couch next to me.

"Is that really a good idea right now?"

"Seems like it."

"You're exhausted, Vann. Why don't you try to get some sleep for a few hours?"

"What if Daisuke calls?" I asked, panicked.

"I'll stay while you rest. You're a freaking mess. And it's going to be another long night." I felt the full weight previous night waft over me. My eyelids were suddenly heavy and ready for some type of hibernation.

"I'm afraid if I go to sleep, I won't be able to get up," I said through a yawn.

"I'm afraid if you don't go to sleep you won't be able to stay up. I'll wake you up—with more of that awful motor oil you call coffee."

"I like strong coffee. I need strong coffee."

"You need sleep. Coffee later." She pointed to the bedroom.

"Just a little while. And you wake me up as soon as Daisuke calls." I rose from the couch and ambled that way.

"I will, now go." I obeyed as my bed offered to swallow me whole upon impact.

* * *

--- May 16th, 9:16 a.m. ---
"Will meet you. Need 45 min. Where?"

Kate heard the chime and toggled over to the message. She glanced up at the closed bedroom door of her best friend who was getting some ferociously needed sleep. Another half an hour would be all she could spare.

"Thank you. Café Dulce at 10 ok?"

Kate realized her text was as curt and to-the-point as the young Japanese doctor and smiled to herself. She could never fake the gushing, erratic behavior of her best friend. Why hadn't he called? Too messy? Worried about who would overhear? Who knows? It had barely been longer than an hour and they were in business. Café Dulce was right by Hama Sushi. They could go over to Maru's car if they wanted. Plus, they made real coffee.

"Ok"

The reply chimed in a minute later and Daisuke's Facebook green dot showing he had been connected went grey. Hmmm, Kate thought, wondering why he would bother to log off after confirming their plans. She didn't reply. He wouldn't see it before they met face-to-face anyway.

* * *

Waking up was like being dragged through tar. I had not dreamed; I had no idea why Kate was waking me up. I was completely disoriented and drained. She tried to fill me in like an amnesia patient while throwing clean clothes from my closet at me. Before I was fully conscious, she was driving my Honda Accord toward Little Tokyo saying we had to meet Daisuke in 15 minutes. That's when I snapped upright.

"What! You talked to him? You said you'd wake me up!" I seethed.

"I didn't talk to him, chill out."

"Chill out! You promised!"

"I made an executive decision. You needed sleep more—"

"What? You can't make an executive decision about my life, not about this."

"Seriously, Vann, trust me. He just replied to your message, and I replied back for you. You're about to meet him at Café Dulce." I pulled up the Facebook app on my phone to check the conversation.

"Café Dulce? I don't even like that place—their coffee is too weak."

"Their coffee is normal. And it's right by Hama in case we need to check out her car together." I read all 15 words of their exchange at one glance.

"Oh, not very talkative, is he?"

"Didn't have to be. See. I didn't want to wake you up for that when you could sleep another half hour and I could just set it up."

"I feel like I just slept for half a century," I said rolling my neck. "Thanks, Kate." She looked straight ahead.

"You needed it."

"No really, You don't know how to take a compliment, but I couldn't do this without you."

"Was that supposed to be a compliment?" She snorted.

"You know, screw you. I'm just saying thanks."

"That's a funny way of saying it." She laughed again.

"Ugh! I am being such a bitch!" I groaned. "I'm sorry; I'm just so tired."

"Well, please don't treat this guy like a bitch. We don't want to piss him off."

"Oh my god, how will we know who he is?" I grabbed her arm panicked.

"He'll probably call you when he gets there so he can find you."

"How do you know?"

"He seems like a level-headed guy. That would make sense."

"It would, you're right. I'm so not level-headed; even on a good day."

"And that's why you have me."

"I would say thanks, but you know." We were both smiling for the first time.

"You're welcome." She said like it was hurting her to do it. She really sucked at accepting any kind of appreciation. This was a breakthrough.

I didn't need to know what he looked like. In a sea full of Asians stuffed in the coffee shop on a Sunday morning, I recognized him right away.

"That's him." pointed to a young man in scrubs walking up outside of the café.

"Oh right, the scrubs. Good one."

"No, it's the eyes. I'd know those deep brown eyes anywhere." He looked just like Maru. Even their hair was the same two-inch faux hawk. Same build and slender nose, too. When he reached for the door handle, it was with her hands. Those were my hands; the ones that go on me. I felt my chest tighten and tried to focus. His jaw was a little longer and lips weren't as full, but the man gazing over the crowd for a familiar face was Maru, no doubt.

"Daisuke!" I called crossing over to him at the back of the line. I reached my hand out to him. "I'm Vann. Thank you so much for meeting me." He took my hand in both of his and bowed his head with the slightest of pauses before bringing it back up. I knew that the Japanese bowed to show respect and Buddhists bowed in gratitude. Whatever his intentions, I was instantly and deeply moved by his warm gesture of acceptance.

"As am I," he said with authenticity in his eyes. I resisted a deep urge to hug him.

"This is my friend, Kate." I gestured toward her. They shook hands, but no bow. Daisuke held her gaze a little longer after the handshake and I swear I saw her blush or something coquettish for her. Was she swooning?

"Can I get you two a coffee while you find us a table?" Kate asked, ever the sensible one.

"Green tea if they have it," he said reaching for his wallet.

"No, I got it," I said. "Something dark for me." I handed her my card.

"Straight espresso, V?"

"Shot in the dark. Straight." She turned and headed to the back of the line as we moved in on a table that still needed to be wiped down.

"This ok?" The table was small and round with only two chairs.

"Sure," he said swinging a vacant chair around from an adjacent table.

"I can't believe we haven't met in eight years. We really should have tried to get together before now," I said, my eyes lingering on his folded fingers on the table.

"Has it been that long? Maru didn't...share many details."

"You really look just like her. I was worried about how I would know you, but I knew you right away."

"That's good, because I was just looking for your Facebook profile picture." We laughed. My profile picture was of Grover, belly up, showing his teeth like a smile.

"Well thanks again for agreeing to meet me."

"How are you concerned about Maru's safety; is she ok?" He stiffened a little.

"Well, I don't know really. That's what I was hoping you could help me with."

"How so?"

"She didn't come home after work last night." I told him the whole story: the conversation with Katsu, the car, the cops and how we came up with the idea of contacting him. While I laid out the story, his face became more and more grave, but he did not interrupt. By the time I finished, Kate sat down with our drinks.

"I thought maybe she had contacted you or your parents." I shook two packets of Sugar in the Raw into the darkness of my drink.

"Vann, I'm not sure what to tell you." He wrapped his hands around the warm tea mug but did not drink it. "I spoke to Maru a couple weeks ago. I'm very confused, here." He looked down into his mug for answers.

"Did she say something when you talked to her?" Kate asked, touching his arm. I shook my head 'no' at her knowing touching in Japanese culture was basically forbidden for strangers. She gave me a confused look on her face. Although the muscles in his forearm twitched, he did not react.

"Yes, she did." He looked up at me, through me, just like she had done at 9:30 AM the previous morning. It seared and comforted at the same time, like a mug of hot tea. "She said she was leaving L.A."

Chapter 6

I strode up to Hama Sushi hoping the line wasn't too long at 3:30 on a Tuesday afternoon. I was on my way from class to my apartment where I needed to do some serious crunch work on my thesis. And what better brain food than raw fish to churn out brilliance on cultural algorithms source codes? I wanted to change the world. Or at least the way people access and manipulate information processing on the internet. But that would be after I got something down the hatch. I hadn't eaten anything since breakfast yesterday or so, and this would have to get me through the night—and maybe until lunch tomorrow depending on the how much of my stipend was left in my account.

Pulling on the door, I looked past the line for my spot at the sushi counter, the second from the end. When the hostess approached me, I pointed to the empty chair and showed myself over. She smiled and nodded toward the counter. I slung my purse over the back of the chair and pretended to look at the menu. I knew what I wanted, always the same thing in the same spot. I marked a 1 beside California roll and yellow tail roll and feigned reading the list until she backed in behind the counter rolling a stainless-steel cart of restock supplies.

I straightened then relaxed, desperately trying not to look desperate. I couldn't help it. I was captivated, which was foreign and out of control for me. Predictability suited me best. Men were so easy: "Feed me. Fuck me." That's all they need. How hard can that be? But this was something else. Like electric satin in my senses.

She turned and looked at me like she already knew I was there. I saw her forehead relax and her eyes disappear in the softest smile. She squared up to me, pressed her palms and bowed slightly.

"Welcome to Hama Sushi. How may I help you?" Her voice unfolded like layers of caramel over me. I felt stupid, but this guttural response was beyond my control.

"The usual, thanks." I said low, like a secret.

"California and yellow tail?" I nodded and handed her the card. She took it in both hands in prayer pose and bowed again. It was so strange to me. The master's degree, the rent, the bullshit all faded away over a tuna roll like freak show magic. See her cut the fish; see her roll the fish; abracadabra! Hypnotized.

I watched her hands closely through the glass. Quick swish of the knife, a slow and deliberate fold. Like a pulsing heartbeat. I don't even know whose sushi she was making, but it was sexy as hell. And I'm certain I never would have noticed, never thought twice about how sushi was made if it wasn't for her; all of her, which she poured into her work and pushed across the counter to me.

"What's this one?" I asked turning the plate to look at the character she had made in spicy mayonnaise sauce beside the yellow tail roll, a masterpiece itself. She smiled broadly and looked over her shoulder at the doorway to the kitchen. She leaned over the counter, turned the plate the right way.

"Call me," she said, smothering me in caramel again.

I realized I was holding my breath when she started talking to another customer down the counter. My god, I was crazy. Her presentation characters had been a flirting game: "funny girl," my name, her name, "beautiful," "sweet" or "sweetness," she had all used before. But this was for real. This was a request—a pick up line. What was I thinking? I smeared a chopstick of California roll through the symbol. Not that anyone would know what it said, except the staff there, and about half the guests; ok two-thirds of the guests. This was in the heart of Little Tokyo.

I couldn't look up. I kept my head down, left hand over my eyebrow like I was hiding somehow. This was too much. I wasn't gay, had never been with a woman. I'm not saying I hadn't fantasized about it, but I never thought about acting on it. But this chick was so hot and amazing with her hands. It wasn't temptation; it was inevitable.

I watched her work through a couple of items on the menu with another customer and glanced away quickly when she cut her eyes toward me smiling. My mind started playing the usual tricks on me, telling me this was impossible. I'm straight; I date men; slept with six of them, unless you count Drake Bale, my prom date that came early, way early.

I had four decent orgasms not manufactured by self-service, which was not much but more than some women muster in a lifetime. I liked man-sex well enough. I thought of myself as quite flexible, both in the hips and the position. My favorite was a reverse cowgirl, his knees up like handlebars with a reach around if I'm lucky. I'd even done this weird Kama Sutra-like pose with an undergrad boyfriend that was literally like getting fucked upside down and backwards.

I was satisfied by my six pack and ready to settle down now that I almost had my master's, could get that unicorn called 'a real job,' and move out of my lousy apartment. But I was staring at this woman whom I had never seen out of a chef's hat and I'm treading in deep uncharted waters. All cowgirls and Kama Sutras aside, I had no idea what I was doing—or what I wasn't doing for that matter. My mind was flopping like that fish I had just eaten: that will never work, but I could try it; you can't be seriously thinking about this, but you don't want to pass it up. Doesn't everybody try it once? Yes, but you haven't had your two drinks yet. Those hands. You don't know anything about women. Her voice all over me. You want to be a social outcast? Perfect smoothness of her lips. What if you can't find a job or if you do and get fired? The wrestling match ended with 'If it's wrong, why am I feeling this magic?'

It's like that sometimes. Love is just love and didn't come in neat, tidy boxes that look like anything I thought I knew or had planned my whole life. I felt the first shift of the rug being pulled from beneath my feet and looked up to find...not what I expected.

I see myself now at that crossroads and I laugh. I was so afraid of making the wrong choice: find a new sushi joint, stick with your comfort zone; or plunge headlong into whatever craziness lay ahead. I could never be sure, never.

I wrote my number on the back of my receipt, folded in in half and dropped in her tip jar. I slung my purse over my shoulder as I headed for the door; I did not look back.

She called me the next afternoon, not even 24 hours later. We made a date for Sunday afternoon. She would pick me up but wouldn't say where we were going. I began to obsess about what to wear, how to smell, my hairdo, make up or not. Men were easy to prep for: dress, but barely, perfume, make up and an up-do that shows off your kissable neck.

Somehow that just didn't seem right. I wasn't wearing sweatpants and a T-shirt but had no idea what the in-between might be. I was nervous. I checked the internet to boost my confidence, but most of those Lesbians were either wearing an evening gown or sensible pants suit. The best I could do was a peasant blouse, cutoff shorts, thong sandals, lip-gloss, and sweet pea body splash. I couldn't resist the up do; I have a fabulous neck. It was still me, just magnified. I didn't go to the grocery store dressed like this, but I certainly didn't go to the club either. It would have to do.

She picked me up, on time, and took me to Sunset Beach for a picnic. A Thai picnic. Being fed off chopsticks is sexy. Forks seemed lame all of a sudden. I might eat all of my food with chopsticks, chicken legs and wedge salads alike, from then on.

She could tell I was completely lost and was deeply kind on that first date. I fumbled horribly, rapid-fire asking questions, not giving her time to answer before giving my own opinion or asking another one. She would smile and listen like it was the most interesting thing she'd ever heard. I began to wonder about her English skills with how little she talked until I realized I wasn't giving her a chance.

I'm sure it was a beautiful day, delicious food and all that. I was too nervous and equally entranced to notice anything, but her hands and few words chopped frequently by my own braying. When we finished eating, she meticulously packed away the leftovers and utensils. I had no idea sushi chefs went under ten or so years of training, and she was making more than I would if I hadn't gone to grad school. I didn't yet know the care and intention she put into every action, not as a part of her occupation, but a part of who she was, her religion and culture. I was aware that I was watching something sacred—tucking chopsticks and napkins into a bag.

I sat cross-legged, watching her intently. She laid out along her side and propped her head up.

"You have so much life," she said. I couldn't tell if it were a compliment, a teasing, or just bad grammar. I didn't care; it was the most beautiful thing I'd ever heard. I wanted to have so much life. I wanted all this. I wanted everything.

She didn't try to kiss me when she dropped me off. I was appalled, or disappointed. I had to keep reminding myself she wasn't some guy trying to calculate how many dates it would take to get me in bed. But I wanted to be kissed. I wanted to know the softness of those lips, to finally feel her hands on me instead of watching them float like a butterfly and sting like a bee. She opened the door for me. I stood so close to her I could feel warmth from her body in the cooling threads of evening. When it was obvious I wanted more, I grabbed her hand and kissed her cheek in a rush.

"I had a nice time, Maru. Thank you for taking me out."

"You? Why not you?" Yeah, why not me?

"I didn't know if I was your type," I tried to play it off. She smiled anyway.

"I didn't either, Vann Townsend." She pulled my hand up and kissed the back. Sweet, harmless and dead sexy how she held my eyes. "But I'm glad I did."

"Me too." I said faintly, but she was already walking around to her side of the car.

"See you again?"

"Yes! Soon!" Not trying to look not desperate anymore. She gave a short nod and disappeared into her Eclipse.

It was a private party. I was excited but couldn't tell anyone. It's like being in the closet, with the most fabulous wardrobe I can't show off. I didn't really have anyone to call about the most exciting date I'd had since, ever. Maybe my sister, but that would be awkward calling her up out of the blue—"you'll never guess what..." Besides, she was so far up my mom's ass which would bring god-knows-what to my doorstep. TMI for classmates and no way I was bragging about it to my fellow interns at Anthem. It was just us in whatever white-hot mess was about to ensue.

Deciding I had been a coward, I called her for our next date to see a matinee show the following Wednesday at the intimate Skiptown Playhouse in Melrose Hill. Trying to fit something into my school and work schedule and her mostly evening shifts was tricky. We had to be creative and flexible, if not willingly unrealistic.

I had no expectations after our first date; how could I? I didn't know what to expect. But I was determined to make her understand my intentions to go to the next step, whatever it was.

When she picked me up for the second date, I casually let her in my apartment and pretended to put the last touches on my lip gloss.

"Almost ready," I said. I grabbed my purse from a hook on the door behind her. I gathered all the nerve I had and planted one on her mouth. My eyes were clenched shut; my hand was squeezing hers too hard. It was awful, I'm sure. The same time I was busy being a weirdo, her mouth was surprisingly soft and warm, not chapped and bristly. I pulled away abruptly and looked into her penetrating, brown eyes. She held my gaze a moment and said "Ready," more like a statement that a question. A statement loaded like a freighter.

"I think so," I said, answering a question that had settled deep in my gut. I didn't know what I was ready for, but I something broke through my subconscious, finally giving confirmation that whatever this was was beautiful. As if she just felt the same opening within me, Maru took my hand, opened the door and walked us out. It was so simple, so relaxed. Just be here, whispered from around me, wherever here is. Just be.

I barely remember the show, just the feel of her thin fingers between my own resting on my thigh. I watched the pulse in her neck more than the play itself. She would smile, squeeze my hand and look back at the stage encouraging me to take it all in instead of staring at her like a unicorn. Same thing to me, I guess. I'm pretty sure I was jealous that her skin was flawless without even a trace of makeup, the lightest shade of perfect tan. She wore men's cologne, which smelled completely different on a woman, softer and smoother, and completely intoxicating. Her black shock of hair in a faux hawk didn't look gelled, as if it naturally did that. Her chinos and button down made it easy for her to look like a man except for the softness of her features and breasts pulling at the seams in her shirt. I (erroneously/stereotypically) thought Japanese women had beestings for breasts. Not this one. I'd never seen anything like her—may as well have been a unicorn.

After the show, I invited her in for a drink, luring her into my apartment.

"I don't drink," she said, stepped inside and shut the door behind her. "And I don't need an excuse." She kissed me right there, completely taking me by surprise. Her mouth took me in and hands gently gripped my hips, not roving for a bra strap already.

"Oh, don't you? I thought you would think it too forward of me to say 'you wanna come up to my apartment and have sex.'" She smiled and looked away. It was the first time I'd seen her self-conscious at all. "Did I embarrass you?"

"Is that what you want?"

"To embarrass you?"

"No, the other part."

"Sex with you? I don't think anyone has ever actually asked me before. Let's see…" I paused pretending to consider my options. She was smiling, in on the joke, but waiting for an answer no less. I was struck by this gesture of respect and consideration. But sweet Jesus, I was about to cave with ravenous desire. I was already a slip n' slide from the waist down after that kiss and couldn't wait for more of whatever she was wanting my permission to do. "Yes, I think I would very much like—"

She kissed me again, this time matching my lust. I pulled her to the bedroom with my arms around her neck, waddling backward. If being swept off your feet was being picked up by someone four inches shorter than you and lain gently on the bed while having your top removed, then yes, I was swept off my feet by Maru.

She was 1,000 hands sweeping across my stomach, my thighs, my neck, all over all at once. Her mouth followed everywhere her hands had been. It was impossible but felt real all the same. Sensory overload, my back arched and eyebrows knitted with pleasure. Breathing hard like a track star, I grappled blindly with the buttons on her top, under which was another fucking shirt. She barely paused to let me pull them off before landing her mouth in some new and unexpected place that had never known lips: my ribcage, the back of my shoulder, my knee pit—yes, my knee pit.

I'd never been so happy to see a sports bra—easy over the top. But I found myself in limbo there. I'd never handled any bra or looked at breasts in that way before, it was like seeing them for the first time. Or rather, what you always wanted your breasts to look like. At 25, she was full, pert and perfect. All this was happening; I was frozen in it. She felt me halting and found my eyes, as if she knew what had happened. She slowed and straddled my now-naked body, pulling off the bra, barely breaking eye contact. She pulled my hand up to her chest and held it over her heart.

"Don't see. Just know." I felt the pounding in her chest. I felt the pounding in my chest and throbbing between my thighs. I wasn't sure it was real. Who fucks like this? Unknowing, I pulled her hand to my own heaving chest. It was like a thread of hot wire connected us. When she smiled and closed her eyes, I felt an electric burst in my stomach and nearly climaxed on the spot. She didn't make me wait any longer.

It was the wildest all-natural phenomenon I had experienced. After the third orgasm, I cried. After two more, I just held on, no longer able to control the shuddering. She felt me nearing exhaustion and slowly kissed her way up along my arm to my fingertips. She pulled me like a ragdoll on top of her and held me with her whole body.

Chapter 7

"She said she was leaving L.A.," he said.

I felt like I was falling down a well. I stopped breathing. The air around me whooshed, the ground come up, the world above me faded into a pin dot of light and the crowd noise had nearly disappeared. I tasted metal or blood in my mouth; my ears were full of water. I turned sweaty and sick.

"She's going to pass out," I heard Kate say from a long way away. My limbs were as useful as wet paper. I couldn't gain purchase on the world slipping from me. Just as I was ready to let go of the immense heaviness of consciousness, Kate slopped a wet napkin on my face, chest and arms.

"Vann?" She repeated. "Vann, it's ok." I was aware that bits of the paper napkin stuck to my face. The whooshing and falling stopped, and light returned to my surroundings.

"Vann, are you ok?" Dab, dab. The spectacle I made at the café ensured I would never go back there.

"Water," I croaked. She handed me the cup she had been soaking napkins in. I drank it anyway washing away that bizarre taste.

"Are you ok?" Daisuke asked.

"What did you say?" I asked, still reeling.

"I asked if you were ok."

"No, before that." I gripped the sides of the café table with both hands like it was a playground sit-n-spin, but I was the only one spinning. He hesitated.

"I said that my sister told me she was leaving L.A." A new wave of nausea hit and something like what I thought a heart attack felt like in my chest.

"I think I'm going to be sick." I lay my face down on the cool tiles on the café table.

"Maybe we should go outside," Daisuke said, his eyes darting between the exits.

"No, no. It's ok. She'll be ok. Just give her a minute," Kate said.

"How do you know? She looks worse."

"She did something similar when our boss died unexpectedly in a car wreck a couple years ago. This girl does not like bad news."

"I'm right here," I said indignant. I turned my head for the other cheek to cool.

"This is bad news?" Daisuke last. "I don't understand." I pulled my face off the table and squared up to him completely drained.

"It means, she left L.A. without me." The tears that streamed across the bridge of my nose turned sharply changing direction as I rose. "It means she left me."

"That's bad," Kate said. She squeezed one of my hands and stuffed the other with more napkins she had dabbed to my face and chest.

"Did she say," I sucked in more air, "anything else?"

"That doesn't make any sense," Daisuke said.

"Did she say where she was going?" Kate said slowly, bring us back on track.

"She made it sound like this was something she was planning in the future. I had no idea..." he trailed off.

"What happened?" I asked no one.

"She didn't say anything about Vann or seem like anything was wrong. Certainly nothing like this." He gestured across the table indicating me, the mess she left behind.

"So she didn't say where she was going?" Kate brushed napkin bits off me. I swatted her away.

"What happened?" I asked again.

"She didn't say anything that indicated an actual plan. More like an idea she had for 'someday.'" Kate and Daisuke had their own conversation while I curled up inside.

"Did she say why?"

"Something about opening a restaurant, maybe. But nothing concrete."

"Ok, did she tell you what kind of restaurant or a name?" Kate pressed.

"No. I mean, I wish I would have recorded it for you. It was barely a conversation. More like, here's how my week was, what are you doing for the holiday and oh, by the way, I think I'll move away from L.A. and open a restaurant someday."

"Well, that sucks."

"What happened?"

"We don't know, Vann. That's what everyone is trying to figure out." I dissolved into shoulder-shrugging sobs. "Oh, come on. Don't be that way. We'll figure it out."

"Figure out what, Kate? Why my wife walked away from me and our whole life without the fucking decency to mention it to anyone, like me?" I said with venom and saw Daisuke flinch. "I'm sorry Dai. I know this isn't what you signed up for."

"I mostly glad you didn't black out on me." He brushed it off.

"I know you're trying to be sweet, but this is messed up. I am a wreck right now."

"Hey, Vann. Take it easy." Kate looked around at people who had taken notice and rubber-necked at the shit show. I embarrassed them, but there was no stopping the train wreck.

"How is it possible to leave everything you know behind and just disappear? Who does that?" I babbled. "I know her. I know her. We aren't like this. We're different. This is not her. Something happened. Something happened. What happened?"

"Is this helping?" Kate asked. "I don't know how this is helping?"

"Is what helping?"

"Asking what happened over and over, V. You've got to get it together." I could see Daisuke dying at the table.

"What, like there a few lines of code that will clear all this up? Jesus, Kate. I'm freaking out right now—I'm entitled!" I said entirely too loudly followed by more sobs. If there wasn't anyone looking before, they were now.

"You don't know anything else?" Kate asked him.

"No, I'm sorry. I really don't." They weren't even talking to me anymore.

"Do you think she would have contacted your parents?" He lowered his eyes and shook his head.

"They don't really...talk."

"Oh, weird. Ok. Anyone else she might have talked to? Any mutual friends?"

"I'm not sure. I don't think so." Kate leaned across the table and spoke softly.

"Did she mention...you know...someone else?"

"I'm fucking right here, and I can fucking hear you. Don't act like I'm not here. I already told you, no. Not that. No way." Which was ridiculous, but I was so far beyond rationality by that point, there was no saving me.

"Ok. That's it. I'm getting her out of here." Kate said. Daisuke relaxed. "I'm really sorry about this." She pulled up on my arm.

"I'm sorry I couldn't be more help."

"No really, you were, and so sweet."

"Are you fucking kidding me? Are you hitting on him?" I'm sure I looked like a drunk asshole, slurred speech, weaving, the whole bit. She snapped my wrist taut like a rope pulling me close to her face.

"You're acting like a bitch. I'm not letting you do anything else you'll regret here," she spit in my ear. I collapsed back in the chair. "Really Daisuke, she's not usually like this. I'm just glad we didn't file the missing person's report."

"Missing person's report?" He showed alarm as he stood up to leave.

"They said we had to wait 24 hours, which is in a few hours. She did file a statement, which I have no idea what that means, but we'll have to retract it. Anyway, please don't worry about all this. We'll figure it out."

"Just let me know if there's anything I can do to help."

"If you hear from Maru, maybe tell her to call her wife." I was flat rude with that.

"You don't have to do that. We don't want to put you in a bad position with your sister," Kate said, and shot me a hateful glare.

"Vann, I don't know what to say. I only know that you mean a lot to her. You're right, this is very unlike her. I am sorry to be the one to tell you this. She should have."

"She said you were the only man she ever loved," I spewed at him one word after another. "She said you were always so kind. She said...so many...things." I blubbered.

"Awkward," Kate said. "I'll go hide her in her car now."

"No, it's ok. I can't imagine how I would react if someone I obviously cared so much for had betrayed me in such a way." That word, 'betrayed', stuck in my mind. That's what this was. Even cheaters face up when caught. It's Judas who slips into the night to seal your fate. I was betrayed—in the most guttural and bewildering way. He touched my shoulder with those hands, a surgeon's or a sushi chef's hands, precise and firmly gentle. Even deeply deceived, I ached in my bones for her hands on me. "I promise to let you know if she calls. You deserve at least that much from me." I blinked up at him in disbelief of his generosity.

"I don't deserve anything from you, Daisuke. You're the one..." I stopped, not knowing what to say. They were so alike in so many ways—I saw so much of her in him. The right words were snatched from me. "You've been a great help."

Kate handed him the collapsed paper panty from her coffee cup. "You can call me if you think of anything." She was definitely flirting. She gave my brother-in-law her phone number, but I was in no mood to fight it. I saw them smiling softly at each other and knew I was in the way of something. "S'go, V."

Daisuke moved through the gaping crowd to the door of the coffee shop I would never be back to. Kate hauled me out by the elbow, giving pathetic looks to the onlookers as we passed.

I was quiet in the car as she drove the couple blocks to Hama, which was just stirring for the upcoming lunch crowd. She put it in park in the back of the lot and sighed heavily into the steering wheel.

"That went well, don't you think?" she said, and turned to look at me.

"I am so sorry. I was such an ass." Just as I thought tears would run out, they came again, quivering in my eyelids. "I don't even know what just happened."

"Nothing good, Vann. This is really bad, babe. Real bad." She started to cry, and I remember cocking my head to the side a little thinking 'never thought I'd see that. "I'm so sorry, so, so sorry," she said. She reached across the seat with a hug of all things. I bawled, twisting both my arms around her, letting it all come apart.

"We just got to…figure this thing out. It'll be ok, ok?" She tried to soothe me, I shook my head 'no' in her chest, knowing it would never be ok. Not for me, I would never be the person I was at 9:30 yesterday. I was already someone else—I didn't like her already. She was mean and didn't want other people to be happy, ever.

"What happened? What's happened to me?"

"I don't know, V. I don't know if we'll ever know." She pulled me back and looked into my eyes like a parent comforting and inconsolable child. "We just go from here, ok?" I nodded, obeying. I dug more fast-food napkins from the console and blew my nose. "Ok." She patted my shoulder like she just realized she had been touching me and came to her senses.

"You have to drive now, ok? We have to get her car home." I looked at her like 'how are we supposed to do that, pick it up and carry it'?

"You'll have to drive your car since you can't drive standard. I'll drive hers back to the apartment. Then we'll go visit the Lieutenant and tell her what's happened. And I think you should call in for work tomorrow."

"Work tomorrow?"

"Yeah, you know. Your job. You need to call Marty and tell him you're not coming in tomorrow." I nodded again. "Can you drive? Are you ready?"

"Just give me a minute." I peeled myself out of the car and went over to the Mitsubishi. I let myself in and sat in the passenger's bucket seat. I could smell her—and fishiness from her work uniform. Her wallet in my hands felt heavy, so heavy. Her phone was cold on my thigh. It wasn't her, but it

was. And it was all I had. No tears; they were all
gone for now.

Chapter 8

I woke up alone the next morning feeling like I'd run 100 miles the night before. I have a friend who has actually run the distance and when she finished, she looked better than I felt. I unclenched Maru's pillow from between my knees where it had made a lousy replacement for the real thing.

I would rather have been sitting in traffic on the way to the financial district, even if it was just past Little Tokyo. Instead, my stomach was a sailor's knot: heavy and twisted beyond all recognition of an internal organ. Grover briefly raised his head, snorted at me, then flopped down on the bed. I pulled the covers up to my chin and blinked. It was the best I could do.

Blink, breathe, blink and breathe again.

Lieutenant White was a real champ when I explained that no, I wouldn't be filing a missing person's report after all and I was, in fact, just a jilted lover and sorry to have wasted her time and thank you again for your compassion and generosity...

I stopped by Hama between lunch and dinner and quizzed the staff from both shifts—completely pointless. My Japanese was little more than reckless, and their English mostly comprised nods and smiles. Katsu wasn't there and didn't answer his phone when I called. I thought very briefly that perhaps it was all a major conspiracy between them against me and dismissed it telling Kate to remind me to call him again the next time she remembered. She probably had a bead on a much more inside source named Daisuke.

When I came home empty with no clues at all, I experienced a sudden burst of energy and went psycho trashing the place. Kate sifted neatly through a few drawers and kept pouring me glasses of cabernet to slow the Tasmanian devil search crew tearing up the apartment.

Looking around at the aftermath, I groaned. Dresser drawers spilled their contents like frothing mouths. The end tables by beds were overturned on the floor. One of the blinds was bent up on the floor. The contents of our closet mounded in the doorway to the bathroom that also looked like a warzone. All that and still no closer to anything than before. I considered moving out and leaving everything behind.

Blink, breathe, blink and breathe again.

We had been robbed. I had been robbed—of my life. My life which I loved and never noticed until it was stolen. Maybe I would go file a report with Lt. White, I laughed to myself. I asked, 'how do I go from here'? These epic questions hung in my threadbare mind, but there was no one to answer. How would I put my own two feet on the floor and walk again? I see myself there, under the covers, immobilized by the throbbing ache in my chest and stomach which had radiated to my useless limbs. I rolled over and closed my eyes—desperate not to see her face in the darkness there. Just a moment without the torment of profound loss. Like your favorite baby doll dropped down the storm drain.

--- May 18th, 9:30 a.m. ---

"Are you there? Please call home."

--- May 18th, 6:47 p.m. ---

"I know you're checking here. Why won't you just call me? What happened? Where are you? So many questions, Ru. Please call home."

--- May 19th, 12:26 p.m. ---
"Your brother told me already. If you were trying to trick me, I figured it out the day after you 'disappeared'. If you were trying to hurt me, nice job. Please call home."

--- May 20th, 12:49 a.m. ---
"I don't know how else to reach you. I don't know why you left. I don't know what I did that forced you away. I don't know anything anymore. You won't talk to me so here I am, talking to you now. I love you. I've loved you since the first California roll you ever made for me—the one that said 'sweet' on the side. And I hate you for doing this to me—to us. Why wouldn't you just TALK to me, give me a chance to understand why you had to leave? Give me a chance to fix things. How do you make someone so crazy for you and just walk away after 8 (EIGHT) years!? I'm so fucked up over this (and the bottle of gin I'm pouring on it). I haven't been to work all week; I can't find you anywhere. I'm passed freaking out, but I did nearly file a missing person's report on you before I met Daisuke. You were right about him. On one hand he kind of ruined my life by telling me you were planning to leave L.A. And on the other, he saved me. I probably would be driving around looking in ditches and alleys right now—because you're so fucked up! Who does that? Your car? Your phone and wallet? What am I supposed to do with your shit? I can't even look at it without breaking down into tears again. Just saying your name haunts me. I don't get it. I have to make up here that maybe you had a secret life. Maybe you went into witness protection. Maybe turning straight girls to the

'dark side' is just your thing and you never loved me. But is it even humanly possible to do what you did even then? I'm sick of trying to figure what I did to you to make you do this to me. You're a fucking coward. You've always avoided talking to me about the shitty stuff, so you don't have to deal with me upset. Well fuck you. You're going to have to deal with me. How could you see me, really see me experiencing you and us and just walk away, Maru? It's so late and it doesn't matter because I can't fucking sleep without you here. You've ruined me. I will never again be that girl you left sleeping beside the place WHERE YOU GO. I'm not even her anymore. I hope you're happy with what you've done with yourself. And I still fucking love you on top of it all. You can still fix this. Please. Call home. V"

* * *

I got up Wednesday, driven from my grave bed by the need for food and liquor. I even went back to work the following Monday. The sun came up; the coffee went down; I went to work; I came back; food went in and I went out. No color, no flavor, sunsets fell flat, music was out of tune. With Maru gone, I felt blank. I couldn't recognize myself. I was a schizophrenic who refused to take her drugs because they say they feel nothing. Except, there was nothing to feel. This was not numbness. That implies there's something stirring underneath. This was void and barren. In, out; black, white; up, down; yes, no: it was all the same.

My life played out like a soundtrack of depressing songs by jilted women. "My Lover's Gone," by Dido; "You Were Meant for Me," by Jewel; "Don't You Remember," by Adele—they were my songs now. I owned them with my soul and tears.

After a month, I quit checking her phone or looking on Facebook for her to sign in. I washed her pillowcase, smeared with my mascara. Kate and I hit the Pink Taco after work once. I had a few too many Long Island iced teas and called in the next day.

--- June 24th, 12:26 p.m. ---
"Home, hung over today trying not to miss you. Do you feel anything? I can't feel anything. Even though it scares the shit out of me, I think it's where I'm supposed to start again, without you. I thought maybe...I don't know what I thought. I still love you. I would quit if I knew how. You were my sun and moon too."

After another month, I laid my ring on the entry table next to her long-dead phone and wallet. I stared at the interwoven layers of sterling silver that made up the band. It seemed like a farce. She had taken hers with her. Why?

I cancelled all her services: phone, subscriptions, gym membership. She had not touched our bank account which contained a considerable sum of her money, and it didn't feel right to close it and take the money. Same thing with the useless car I couldn't drive. I didn't know whether to sell it, donate it or set it on fire. She left the keys in it like it was free for anyone walking by to drive it away. I would have thought she was carjacked and being held hostage or something crazy. And the more I tried to make sense of it, the more it seemed incomprehensible.

I felt like I was settling the affairs of the deceased, as if she had died. I went through the mechanics of our relationship like nothing more than a checklist of accounts and assets. I had gone as far as I could go alone, but her damn Mitsubishi stared at me through the window from the street, nagging.

Maybe because I was lonely; maybe because I wanted to see her again; maybe I wanted to avenge my tattered heart. Whatever it was, I invited Daisuke to the apartment to pick up a few of her family things—anything he wanted really. I would give away what I couldn't use or wear, I explained, but I wanted him to have first shot.

When I answered the door, my heart sank. I wanted him to look less like her, but he was freshly shaven, wearing a button-down and dark jeans with loafers, and I swear, her cologne. They could have been twins. I was instantly homesick in my own home.

"Thank you for coming," I mumbled, trying my damnest to not have a repeat of our last encounter. "Welcome to the home we shared." I had left the place mostly like she left it as if she were on a trip— a sudden, long and unexpected trip.

"Thank you, Vann." He stepped in. "I've actually been by before. I think you were at work one day when I was visiting Maru." I recognized the bronzed tone of her voice.

"Of course. Well, make yourself at home...again." I noticed he put his phone and wallet on the table by the door, right next to hers. My heart squeezed, but I was grateful he wouldn't be checking his phone every 20 seconds like 95% of the rest of the population would have. I padded off in my socks to retrieve the box of her things from the office.

I set it on the coffee table in front of him. "Just some cooking things I have no idea how to use, some trinkets from her altar, a few of her books and the letters...have you heard from her, Daisuke?" He looked up from cautiously rifling through the artifacts of his sister and fully took me in.

"Not yet." He squeezed my hand, an overt gesture of compassion. "Not yet but she will call. She always does."

"Does she?" He nodded. "Has she done this before, Dai?" When he paused, my mind raced and tears welled.

"Disappeared? Yes. But not like this."

"What happened the other time?" Who had she left in her wake last time? I thought I knew her and didn't think it possible for her to do something like this. What did it say about me that she was a repeat offender? Had I ever known my own wife at all?

"There was no one. She just went off grid."

"She wasn't in a relationship?"

"Right, it was more like she was hiding than...than disappearing."

"Hiding? From what?" He thought for a moment.

"Maru is a private person, even from me. I'm not sure I always understood, but it was mostly like she just wanted a reset or some unfiltered self-examination time."

"How long?"

"A few weeks, a few months." I made a confused look.

"How many times has she done this, Dai?" I asked with alarm.

"A few. After high school, a couple times in culinary school. But it hasn't happened for a long time. It stopped, really, when she met you."

"I guess so. I mean, I've seen her withdraw from social life for a couple weeks a few times in eight years, but I didn't think anything of it—well, not until now. What does it mean?" He looked down.

"There's no answer, Vann. Maru is...complex."

I nodded, urging him on. "Is there something you're not telling me?"

"I'm not sure that there is anything I can tell you—not that will comfort you any."

"I'm so far beyond comfort, Dai. I'm just trying to move on. You and I probably know more about Maru than anyone. I'm just hoping to understand this...this craziness—for my own sanity."

"I remember the first time Maru shut us all out. I remember how hurt I was. I can't imagine how much more intense it would be for you."

"For me? I'm not related to her. I was just fucking her."

"I think you know it was more than that for you." Who was this man? How did he penetrate so deeply with his words?

"Yes...but it's what I have to keep telling myself so I don't turn into that crazy woman at the coffee shop." I tried to laugh. He didn't, but I could see his eyebrows relax and face soften.

"Whatever happened at Café Dulce was painful for all of us. We should have had that conversation in private, really. I think you were justified in your...reaction."

"You're too kind. No one is justified in acting like that."

"Who can say? Certainly not Kate or me. Or any of those people staring at the spectacle you made." He smiled then. "There is no way for us to know fully what you were experiencing or how we ourselves would react if we experienced the same thing. I mean from the beginning of your relationship up to how it ended."

"Do you really think it's over? Do you think she's gone for good?

"That's not what I should have said."

"It's what you meant. And it's ok if that's what you think, Dai."

"I think she loved you—"

"But not enough." He cut his eyes to me.

"Perhaps as much as she could, as much as she knew how."

"I believe she loved me, I truly do. This is all just so confusing… and shocking. I feel paralyzed. Like, do I move on; do I wait. Do I look for her; do I lay low?"

"I don't know if you'll be able to find her. I think that's the point of these things."

"I found you." I squeezed his shoulder. It was firm but relaxed.

"Ahh, yes you did. It helps if you know where to look." I felt my own hand drifting down his back. I became aware that I had moved into him, way past the "Tokyo halo," that expansive personal space Japanese people maintained. It was weird. I knew I wasn't supposed to, but my body was out of my control and advancing on this man I lured to my apartment, who was comforting me and trying to be kind. He looked and smelled and felt like the one thing in the world I loved and missed the most. He didn't back away, halt or show any signs of being disturbed by my sudden incursion. He watched me closely, looking amused, as if he were curious about what I might do next. So was I. I looked at my own hand like it was some wild animal that was sweetly stroking with the thumb. My brain knew it wasn't her, but my senses thought it was and craved the smell and taste and sweet, smooth feel of her skin. Instinct had taken over.

Our body heat collided, and I braced for what was coming next. He pressed the back of my hand like pulling the reins on a wild horse.

"I know you miss her, Vann…" I nodded in complete agreement as I landed my lips over his and completely dissolved like a well-placed Klonopin.

I couldn't apologize. I wasn't sorry; I was warming up. Tingling in long-dormant body parts fired outward jarring me from the muck of misery I had waded through for two months. My leg crossed over both of his straddling him on the couch.

"Vann," I heard him say again, this time definitely halting.

"Shhh," I said covering his lips with a few fingers. "It's ok."

"You don't want—"

"I don't want a lot of things," I said kissing his neck. God, he smelled so fucking good; I felt drunk. When I felt his hands on my hips, firm but not pushing me away or pulling me in, my brain finally registered what the flesh had already known. Any resistance I had evaporated when I felt those hands on me. I was ravenous. My pelvis thrust into him, and I felt him stiffen through his jeans.

"Vann." He said more softly, fighting surrender. I kissed him again, pushing him further into the couch. My fingers curled into his substantial pectorals. There wasn't anything in my head saying, 'you shouldn't fuck your wife's brother,' or even, 'you'll regret this later.' That would have been sensical and there was nothing that made sense about any of this. My brain said things like, 'no breasts—of course,' and 'oh, haven't felt one of those in a while' when I registered he had a full-on erection. Eight years or eighty, it wouldn't have mattered. I knew what to do with one of those and my body felt the same feral desire to be fucked right then.

"I want you," I dripped into his ear grinding my hips over him.

"I'm not her," he barely got out, but his pelvis was thrusting against me and those hands definitely pulling me in.

"I said I want you." I looked all the way into him; his eyes had grown lazy and glassed. I gave an inebriated smile, smoothing my lips. When I kissed him, I asked for his permission this time. He knew it to; it was all there. All the madness, all the want and need came through when I opened my mouth over his and waited for him to come in.

He was all man: the tender firmness, the sheer simplicity and straight-to-the-point urgency. I was half-naked before I even got his shirt open. His mouth was soft on me while his hands were unyielding on my breasts. His body pulsed, responsive to my thrusts; he took in everything he wanted. I wanted to be taken; I wanted to feel something again.

We backed into the wall so hard my head knocked into him. He jerked up.

"Oh, god. I'm sorry," he said holding my face like a fragile bowl. I grinned and went for the button on his jeans. I slipped my hand into his boxers and pulled him back onto me. He moaned in my ear. I felt a swift spike of reality realizing he was big, at least 8 inches of solid, pulsing man shaft. He probably wasn't that large, but certainly bigger than anything I had played with in the past decade, which was mostly G-spot finders or two very well-placed fingers of an artist. I wondered where I was going to put all that when he lifted me up the wall. Surprised, I braced for impact. He held me with one arm and most of his body while he stripped my panties over my ass with the other kissing my neck almost through. His hand coursed quickly through my unkempt pubic patch and hit pay dirt between my thighs. He was definitely a surgeon. I felt him smile in my neck as I went limp against the wall. Those fucking hands. If I was going to be embarrassed about my lack of personal manicuring it was too late. I couldn't care if I tried.

All those weeks of anger and hurt and longing and grief rushed to the surface and broke open. I felt voracious and woozy. It was surreal. I had some third-party moment where I could see all this happening—see myself panting into his chest, my arms around his neck, one leg around his waist, the other barely on the ground, every square inch of my body throbbing into him, him who was barely undressed. I needed this really bad. It was the only way to let all that shit out, if only for that moment.

I convulsed, ready to climax in his hand. To my complete bewilderment, he pulled me away and into the bedroom. His arm was like a slingshot whipping me wildly sideways on the bed. In a flash, I had gone from near explosion and sweet release to groping wildly for my bearings in the sheets. The look on his face was intense. I looked up at him, still reeling. He pulled his arms out of his shirt. The guy was seriously sexy. I don't know when he found time to work out, but he was plenty built with impressive shoulders. His skin was smooth and bronzed; the only visible hair on him was wisps snaking down into his boxers which I gladly pulled off. Apparently, we had both been dripping wet.

We hung there briefly fully in the moment. He took me in, I checked him out, each watching the other do the same. He leaned over me with a deep kiss. His hand gripped my hip and I pushed myself up to him. That feeling of skin-on-skin was intoxicating. He was heat; he was pulse. I was mad with hunger. I took his cock in my hand and felt my nipple fully enveloped by the wetness of his mouth. The surge of sensation made me gasp and let go. He thrust it against me, throttling my clit. I pulled his hips in harder, my back arching.

And this probably is way too much detail, but it was the first time in nearly a decade I'd slept with a man, and I remember every detail like it was my first time—which didn't have any details, really. And this was so maniacally different than anything I had experienced or was likely to feel again. He wasn't just trying to get me off so he could feel like accomplished sex god. This was more complex; this was blindingly intense. He was trying to make us climax at the same time. I'd never even considered the possibility of such a feat for straight sex. From what I remembered, I would hope the guy could last long enough for me to get one in after he unloaded. It wasn't 'ladies first' or a foreplay climax. This was something else completely. Each time I was on the verge, he pulled back or shifted or moved so that I wouldn't cum. It drove me completely crazy until I was aching for him with every pore on my flesh.

He locked into my gaze as he pressed himself into me. My eyes squeezed shut and I hissed feeling like I had just been split in half. I grabbed two fistfuls of sheets and my eyes watered. It had been so long, it felt like the same stinging shock of the first time. But this was no high school boyfriend—this was a very full-size man bursting through my hips.

He laced his fingers through one of my hands and propped himself up with the other. He pulled back a bit relieving some of the pressure and waited for me to start breathing again. "You ok?" he said with such tenderness I thought he might stop right there. I pulled his face into mine, kissing him fiercely, sure I busted his lip. I squeezed my calves around his butt forcing him deeper into me.

He flattened himself against me until I could feel him taking me completely over. It was both of us in our entirety tangled up and drilled down into the blade and chalice. Sure, we both knew it was raw fucking, but it was also sacred. He stayed deep and pulsed shallow. It felt like my physical body was slipping away as I neared climax and hoped like hell he wouldn't stop me this time. My head pressed forcefully back into the bed; my back arched until I thought I would break. He felt me quicken and thrust deeply. I was already rolling into a full screaming orgasm, pulling him by the hair, when I felt him plunge nearly through me and explode in my pelvis.

I couldn't believe what had just happened. He was trembling while I was convulsing. At that point, it seemed so unfair. Men had these puny little three-thrust orgasms that faded faster than a mouse fart. Maybe it was harder for women to climax—hell, some went their whole lifetimes without one—but when they did happen, it was like a full-body seizure bursting with bliss that went on, and on, and sometimes, on yet more. No man screeched obscenities for twelve seconds straight completely oblivious that there is even another person in the room, much less victims surrounding you on four sides of your apartment. If men felt the same thing, would they cry, would they cling, would they hold you so tight you couldn't breathe? Oh, I think, yes. It was Eve's little secret, hidden deep within the garden. Cum all you like, Adam. She'll take quality over quantity any day.

And what struck me somewhere between still whimpering and complete collapse, as completely fucked up as it was to even be thinking such a thing—Daisuke had accomplished the same thing with one as Maru had with five (or six, or more, I admit, sometimes): absolute ecstasy. It was quick and nasty fucking instead of the marathon lovemaking that left me hoarse and sore. I would be sore, but not from back spasms.

And the thing that haunted me most with her was that she would never let me pleasure her. She said making me cum did pleasure her, but it was always about me and a new orgasmic Olympic record. How many, how close together, how far apart, how long, how loud, just as long as we were going for broke, and it was better than the last time. Sometimes I would be way past exhaustion and just clinging. I knew she had orgasms. I could feel her seize or tremble sometimes while she was going to town on me. But it seemed like a minor obstacle in her mission when I really wanted to celebrate that

I had made her cum too, or at least stop and acknowledge that we were on the same team. But our sex was about me, my orgasms, my satisfaction. And while that was all great—fucking incredible most of the time, I was dumbstruck as Daisuke rolled to my side how much he had been there with me. I had no idea how much I missed pleasing someone else with my body. He had gone to impossible lengths to make sure it had been about both of us.

I felt astonished and depleted when I backed myself snuggly into his frame. I pulled his arm over like the corner of a blanket and slid into sleep.

Chapter 9

I woke up maybe an hour or a week later; it was hard to tell. Daisuke was draped over me still passed out. I was throbbing in my crotch. I could still feel quite sharply where he had been inside me. I could smell the sweet-salty mix of sweat, flesh and sex. And then the second thoughts came in. What had just happened here? What was wrong with me? Had I planned this when I asked him to come over? How could I do such a thing to her? To him? And sweet Jesus, when would that throbbing ease up.

I became acutely aware that we were completely naked sprawled recklessly across the bed. I'm sure it was what Eve felt when she realized she had been naked all that time—I mean, how can you not know something like that. I had a horrific flash of Maru deciding to come home at that moment and find...this.

"Welcome home, baby," I would say, throwing his arm off and rushing to her. I mean really. How would all that go down?

And then the bad cop started in. Hadn't she been the one that left me so cruelly? I had turned into a barren wasteland, an emotional draught. That was certainly over, literally, I thought, feeling the gush and ooze of sex. I didn't do anything to her. I mean, was this cheating? If a straight girl sleeps with a woman, is she cheating on her husband? So, what about the reverse? And wait, did this mean I was straight again?

Estrogen overflow was still cramming crazy questions into my consciousness when he woke up with a long stretch?

"You awake?" he asked. I nodded and caressed his arm. I seriously wasn't sure what to say or how he was going to react. It was definitely the most awkward post-coital feelings I'd ever had, and there had been some weird ones for sure.

"You ok?" he asked, stroking my shoulder. I nodded again, but still couldn't make eye contact. "Did I hurt you?" He flattened his palm below my belly button like he was trying to feel for himself. I shook my head even though I could still feel every heartbeat pounding out angry between my thighs. "I thought maybe there for a minute, but I wasn't sure."

"Oh yeah, I still feel that." I nodded and giggled a little.

"Oh, Vann, I'm so sorry."

"You don't have anything to be sorry about," I said turning on my side toward him. "That was incredible. I'm just...mmm...out of practice I guess." He smiled.

"So, you've been with a man?"

"A few. Ok, a small handful."

"You don't have to tell me, I just didn't know if..." His voice, his tone, had changed. He was more fluid and open. More American. I wondered if I had projected all those Japanese complexities on him and he was no more Asian than his eyes and skin tone.

"Six, actually. But none like that." I looked away, embarrassed. "How did you...I mean, at the same time?"

"Wow, so you're really not gay?"

"What kind of question is that?"

"Well, I mean, I don't know a lot of…you're just not like Maru, I guess."

"Neither are you," I laughed nervously. "She was a gold star, anyway."

"Gold star?"

"Not been with a man. This is weird, talking to you about your sister like this."

"Can't be any more awkward than…you know…"

"No kidding. What about you. I mean, I've told you all my stats. And you still haven't told me how you did that, anyway."

"Did what?"

"You know. The whole orgasm-at-the-same-time thing. Don't act like you didn't do that on purpose."

"Of course I did. It never worked before, though."

"Seriously? You handled me like you do this every day with like an army of nurses at work."

"Really? You've probably been with more women than I have." I didn't respond. "Oh god, Vann. You haven't been with any other women, have you?" I shook my head. "Wow. I'm guessing Maru got you really messed up."

"Have you every slept with her?" He shot me a look.

"Of course not," he said sharply, and I felt bad. "She's not into guys." I laughed when I could tell he was joking.

"So, you have been with more women than I have."

"None like you, though."

"Of course not. You don't have to try to woo me or something."

"Well, that wasn't fair."

"I'm not sure what's fair about this whole situation actually."

"I was just saying you're exceptionally… different."

"Wow, that's the best complement you had?"

"It wasn't a complement. You're wild, Vann. I could barely keep up with you—"

"Keep up with me? You didn't seem to have any problems pulling me back from like two or three orgasms to set your own pace."

"Well, no. But the women I've been with aren't about to cum in my hand after about 90 seconds, either. You were so...ready."

"I told you I thought I was possessed. It was like I needed you."

"It was like you needed her you mean?"

"I needed to get fucked, I think. So much came out just now. I feel like—released or something."

"I thought I felt something like that. I mean," he leaned closer like he didn't want anyone else to hear. "I felt you orgasm." He seemed pretty surprised he had said it out loud.

"What do you mean?"

"This is bizarre, just talking to you like this."

"No really, what did you feel?" He took a breath.

"Ok, so you are really tight and there was all this pressure. I knew we were both close and..." He realized what he was saying and stopped. I raised my eyebrows to encourage him on. "Well, it felt like a fist or something squeezing me tighter when you started to—you know."

"Fucking freak out."

"Yes, something like that. And I just exploded on the spot. If you weren't cumming, I was going to anyway. How did you do that? I've never experienced anything like it."

"I think you felt my orgasm. I mean I certainly wasn't doing it on purpose."

"Vann, I've never even been with a white girl before. That was seriously the freakiest thing I've ever experienced."

"So, I'm a white girl?"

"Well, the whitest thing in Little Tokyo."

"It was also the freakiest thing I've experienced if you're keeping score at home," I said matter-of-factly. "It was certainly more than just sex."

"What was it? I mean to you."

"Dai, I have no idea what the fuck that was. I'm not even sure if you're ok with it. Much less if I am."

"I don't know, either. It's kind of overwhelming."

"Imagine how I feel."

"That's what I was talking about." Of course he was. Never thinking of himself.

"Who are you?" I narrowed my eyes and moved in closer.

"What do you mean?"

"I mean, you've treated me like a cracked glass, like you're so afraid I'll break in your hands—up until now that is. And now you're all chatty Kathy, Curious George."

"Who?"

"It's an expression. You know Curious George. Come on."

"Yeah, but what's a chatty Kathy."

"You're cracking me up. It just seems like everything you've said up until this very conversation has been so deliberately aimed at trying to preserve my feelings and now it seems like you're someone else entirely."

"I'm sorry?" He asked for clarification as if he had done something bad.

"No, don't be sorry. No, I like you better this way." I slid my arm under his and stroked his back. "I like that you didn't just throw on your boxers and run away like nearly every other guy I've been with. I feel like I can actually talk to you, you know."

"You mean like women?"

"I wouldn't know. I mean, I guess so. What happened?"

"You keep asking that every time I see you." He laughed at his own joke.

"You keep fucking up my world every time I see you." I fake punched him on the arm, but he caught my lazy throw and shook out my fist so that our fingers twined.

"No really, Vann. That was..." he trailed off.

"Wrong?" I cringed.

"Is that what you think?"

"No, well I don't know. I mean, I didn't know what you thought."

"I was going to say 'unexpected'."

"That too."

"Do you think we were wrong to have moved with the moment like that?"

"I think you couldn't have stopped me if you tried. I felt freaking possessed."

"I did try. Well, at least wanted you to know what you were getting into."

"You did not preface that whole craziness with what I was getting into, Dai. That was the best sex I've had in a long time."

"I'm guessing you haven't had sex in a long time."

"Well, no..." I pulled back like I was going to pretend to hit him again. He effortlessly curled my arm against my breasts and held firm.

"No violence." He said in such a way I wasn't sure if he was serious or not.

"I wasn't going to hit, not that it would hurt you much anyway."

"I didn't think you would. Just use your words, ok?"

"I didn't realize you would get so offended."

"I'm not really. I just want to know you, not your reactions when you're feeling like that. Just talk. Especially here."

"Oh, you mean here, in your sister's bed, with your sister's wife." He clinched his jaw. I felt like a shit for saying it.

"That's better."

"What do you mean? That was mean."

"It was words."

"You are very different."

"From her? I told you I wasn't her."

"I found that out, for sure. But I mean, she barely talked to me this much in eight years. Ok, I'm exaggerating, but you know what I mean."

"Yes, I do." He smiled. "It was part of her charm."

"She had plenty of that..." He could tell I was comparing them, but he was just watching me while I drifted into memory. When I saw it, I snapped my eyes back to his. "When I woke up, I was afraid."

"Afraid of what?"

"Afraid that I had fucked up really bad. Afraid that you would regret this and be mad at me."

"Do you think that now?"

"Well not now. Now I'm afraid you'll leave." I wasn't even sure what I was saying. Just words. He kissed me and I felt his eyelashes shutter closed on my cheek.

"I'm still here."

"So, what happens now?"

"I don't know, Vann. This is a lot of firsts for me, here."

"That's for sure. I don't want to go the rest of my lifetime without another one of those, though." I couldn't believe I just said that.

"Is that what we really want? How is this all going to play out."

"I know what you're thinking. I had a terrible vision of Maru coming home just now. How would we...explain that?"

"It's kind of self-explanatory, I think."

"True. I can't believe I'm even thinking about her feelings. After what she did."

"You still love her, Vann." He looked at me like 'how could you not know that'?

"I do. I probably always will. I don't think I have a choice—ever had a choice."

"Love is...unpractical...like that sometimes."

"No shit, Dai. This whole situation is about as unpractical as it gets."

"Maybe not entirely," he said grinning. I got the message.

"Do you think she knew?"

"Knew what?"

"To like, never introduce us. That something like this would happen and that's why we never met all this time."

"I don't think any of us would ever imagine something like this would happen. I thought you were gay and just getting back at her. Why would you sleep with me if you didn't have a reason to hurt her?"

"Is that what you think this is? A revenge fuck?"

"I don't know, Vann. Do you?"

"I know it wasn't that. I know, well, I think I didn't plan this."

"You think?"

"On a conscious level. I wanted you to get her things out of my sight. They made me so...so...desperate. I've been trying not to obsess over being left like a hot rock and having all those things around just reminded me of being a failure."

"You think you were the failure?"

"Something went wrong. I have to cop to that, Dai. But just about any time you find yourself fucking your wife's brother, there's something that has to do with failure there."

"I'm sure that sounds worse than you meant it."

"Not you. Just this situation."

"Now you're trying to flatter me?"

"No! I'm being serious. I did not sleep with you to get back at your sister."

"Then why did you sleep with me, miss?"

"I don't know! You, you are so hot and remind me so much of her." I was really off to the races here and knew that's exactly what he wanted. Alas, I couldn't stop myself. "You smell like her. Your hair, your hands, your fucking hands—they even feel like her on me. You dress like her, and your face, your eyes, those eyes. It's like staring at the thing you want the most but can't have." He was watching me again, curious where we were going this time.

"I saw you and I missed her. My whole body missed her. I kept saying I was possessed, Dai, and I'm telling you, my body was moving independently of my thoughts. Well, at least until all thinking left my body. But then I wasn't thinking anything, just wanting—seriously needing you on me, in me, all that. I sound fucking crazy. Why don't you stop me when I sound fucking crazy?"

"It's not crazy to miss someone like that."

"How are you so stoic? I mean, seriously, what would you say to your sister if she walked in right now."

"I'm not trying to be stoic, by any means. I think I would tell her what happened."

"It would be obvious what happened, wouldn't it? We're lying here, in her bed naked. You're still oozing out of me. I know she hasn't been with a man, but I think she'd figure it out."

"Seriously? It comes back out?"

"Yeah. I forgot about that. Sorry. Sounds kind of gross."

"Not really, I'm just surprised, I guess. I mean, I know a lot of anatomy and never thought about that. I don't mean to change the subject."

"What kind of doctor are you studying to be?"

"Hand surgeon."

"That explains it."

"What?"

"You have great hands."

"Ok? Oh. Oh." He figured out what I was insinuating. "Are you sure it wasn't the idea of her hands you liked so much."

"It was very much your hands I liked. That one-handed against-the-wall trick was amazing."

"I think I just missed the doorway, actually."

"Haha," I said sarcastically. We looked at each other too long. "I didn't know you, Daisuke. I'm not usually like this, really?"

"Like what?"

"Like what? Like a slut, like some uncontrolled sex fiend. I wanted to feel something. I've just been so disconnected this whole time, feeling so alone—so utterly alone. Missing her. Every day."

"I miss her too."

"I'm so sorry. I didn't even think about you losing a sister in all this."

"I understand you were preoccupied."

"But really. What are we going to tell her? You said she comes back; she always comes back."

"I've never seen her gone this long, never like this."

"You don't think..." I sat up suddenly feeling panicked. "She committed suicide?"

"No. Definitely not."

"How do you know? I mean you said—"

"I just know." He pulled my arm down so that I curled into him again. "That's not her thing."

"What's her thing? Running away, breaking my fucking heart?"

"You know this is going to be the same thing for her, right?"

"I guess not. I guess I just imagined her being like 'oh well, you have a nice life' if she ever comes back this way."

"You have to be ready for this conversation, Vann. We have to be ready."

"What do you say? 'I missed you. I fucked your brother'?"

"Yeah, something like that. Something just like that."

"This makes no sense. None of this whole situation makes any sense." I looked up and saw him watching me. "What?"

"You're beautiful," he said.

"You're just saying that because you never slept with a white girl before."

"No. Stop deflecting. You are. And all this…mess, it's amazing."

"You have a strange sense of wonderment."

"I guess I'm just wondering how all this came together to be this very moment. It was just as plausible that this never happened."

"Do you wish it never happened?"

"No. I'm glad I felt that; felt you. Do you?"

"Maybe under different circumstances. I feel bad about pulling you into this. I feel bad about a lot of things."

"So you do wish it didn't happen." He was trying to get me to answer for myself.

"No, I'm not saying that either. I'm saying where were you eight years ago? How did I fall for your sister and not you?"

"Do you think you could be in love with me? Me and not her?" I did think about that one.

"I don't think I could ever see you and not think of her. But going from here—maybe I could love anyone. Certainly you. I'd like to get to know you first. But I do feel that I know you. You're so…expressive. With your body and your thoughtfulness. It's like I've always known you." He seemed mildly surprised. We hung there for a moment, growing weary again from exhausting sex and conversation. I kissed him again and again.

"Can't we just be normal people and make some dinner?" he said and smiled.

"Oh, totally. Do you cook?" I straddled him and massaged my fingers into his pecs. He shook his head, eyes drooping.

"Damn. See if you can get your sister to bring us some sushi," I joked. "Ok, probably too soon." He nodded.

"I'll order us a pizza."

"You are still in college, aren't you?"

"It won't be here for another 45 minutes..." His eyes drifted to my breasts. My hair fell around our faces when I leaned over to kiss him again. He tucked it behind my ear and smiled. He looked so content. I felt so content—if only just then, it was enough.

"I could totally be in love with you." I slid my body down against his. His arms curled snuggly around my waist and we both fell back to sleep.

Chapter 10

And that's kind of how it was for us. Maru's mythical, mystical brother became "Daisuke and me." Certainly not what I was expecting or what I had planned for myself. Then again, none of this whack rotation of planet Earth was anything deliberate. In those obscure and harried days, I was never in control, not once. It was total groundlessness. And for the first time in my life, I wasn't scared to death by not knowing.

While I was with Daisuke's, Maru became someone else entirely. He told me about coming to America when he was eight and she was 13. It was so much easier for him to adapt while Maru stayed on the fringe of any social group. She probably knew what she was from very early for which she further ostracized herself to avoid any potential ridicule.

She had developed virtually no defenses and would not allow herself to get too close or to reveal herself fully to anyone. Not even him. He felt certain she loathed him for how easily he sailed into American life. He picked up the language quickly, fit in with the other Asian boys at school, picked up sports and was good enough to broaden his spotlight; he was even attracted to the socially correct gender.

She would never come out to him, but when he told her he knew and didn't care who she wanted to be with, she softened toward him. He knew that was unacceptable for a self-respecting Japanese person and she deeply appreciated his ability and sheer willingness to be on her side—the outside. She was out of the house before she turned 18 and never came back, ever. They wouldn't have that conversation until he himself was graduating nearly five years later, when he saw her again. As he was telling me this, I thought about my own sister and my heart ached for him. I couldn't imagine walking away from her like that. I'm no big sister of the year. Even though we have hardly anything in common, I still go home a couple times a year and call her at least every week. Ok, every two weeks. But still.

He went on filling in more holes of things I never even realized I didn't know about her. I came to understand that my blissful oblivion about us was purposefully shrouded by her efforts at self-preservation. Replaying whole conversations to him, I saw that she never lied but shrewdly deceived me by construing her (brief) words. I heard him repeating some of the exact things she had said to me—having heard it all before from her—it was chilling.

She was so intensely private, neither of us knew how many girlfriends she had had or women she had been with. He wasn't even sure if she had been with any other women. I assured him without a doubt based on personal benefit of her previous experience.

I told him about the California rolls and brief romance and this woman I (apparently) never really knew but loved so fiercely. She was permanently seared on my soul: her body, her gazes, of course those hands, the clothes she wore, even her fucking sushi I could taste in my mouth every Tuesday. No matter how much I wanted to be something else, at one point I had been wholly hers. I would always bear that yearning to return that sweet ignorance from 9:30 that Saturday.

We were like these wounded refugees of her insolence. Once I came to understand that he was no less left behind than I, we fell in like a deck of cards or entwined pipe cleaners. Whatever it was, we found sanctuary and solace within each other. I could and would tell him anything, seriously anything. I openly compared them; nothing was off limits. For his part, his curiosity was insatiable. The future physician in him quizzed every corner of my physical and psychological consciousness. If I could say anything, he wanted to know everything.

What was it about a merlot that I preferred to a cabernet or Riesling? Did I prefer my Honda to her Mitsubishi just because of the standard transmission or was it the features of the car? Was I a lyrical or beat listener in my music choice? And that was just the usual stuff.

Sex was off the chain, unreal. How much areola stimulation did it take to go from pleasure to nausea? Did I prefer oral sex as foreplay or the main course? I'll never forget once when I had this epic orgasm that lasted like two minutes (or maybe close to 20 seconds, but still a really long time) where I was in grand mal seizure mode and like, no noise came out, but I screamed somewhere in there. He became very animated, thrusting wildly asking if I felt did, did I feel it this time? And fuck if he didn't want a damn answer. Not that I had any option to respond. But that kind of intensity is like trying clap over the sound of two passing trains. Electric fire was exploding through every nerve in my body simultaneously—so no, I didn't feel him feeling my orgasm that time.

Afterward, the complexity of sex leaving us completely exposed, we'd have these long raw conversations about the huge questions in life.

Sometimes I cried; sometimes it was him. We always planned to order a pizza and fell asleep, absolutely exhausted from all that had been laid bare.

Of course, this made for awkward conversation with Kate, who apparently had her own designs on the man she had met at Café Dulce. She chalked it up to being naive about her chances with him and that it was totally FUBAR how much he looked like Maru and no wonder I wanted him. He was the perfect wife.

I admit, she was right. I missed the comfort and feel of breasts against my flesh and in my mouth, but otherwise, Daisuke was the perfect wife. Still, she was hurt and lonely since I was spending so much more time with him than I had with Maru even. I tried not to skip our Thursday dates at the Pink Taco, but if Dai was getting off a shift or had the night off, I jumped at the chance to absorb his rare slips of free time for myself. It would have been way awkward to invite her over to watch movies with us or out to eat, so my time for Kate was carved considerably. I couldn't help but feel bad for ditching her after so swiftly soaking up a guy she was interested in. Nor could I help myself from absorbing him.

Yes, Daisuke and I were friends, the closest kind. Yes, we were fuck buddies. Yes, we were victims of the same defector. We never discussed anything else that we were or might ever be. Ever reminiscent of the first time Maru and I made love: Only don't know. Don't know anything until you know it. And then forget that you ever thought you knew.

It was late—med-school late. We were in the middle of one of these post-coital benders on the neuroses of people who preferred the simplicity and tidiness of rice (me) versus the wild unpredictability of lo mein noodles (him) when the home phone rang. The home phone rang. Long after any telemarketer dare ever make a home call. I froze, fearing the worst. I knew it was her, just knew it. The whole room tilted and started swirling. It was Café Dulce all over again.

"Do you want me to answer it?" he asked, already knowing what I was thinking.

"No!" It rang again. "She'll know."

"She's going to know, Vann." He looked at me like 'we talked about this'. "You have to answer; she knows you're home at 1 a.m." I sat up and reached out for the receiver. I bit my lip and frowned at the caller ID.

"Where's she calling from?"

"Home," I said completely confused. It rang again and was perilously close to going to voicemail.

"Here?" I shook my head.

"My home." I pressed the "talk" button on the receiver and slowly brought it to my ear. Bracing myself, I barely squeaked out "Hello?"

"Vann? Is it you?"

"Yes, it's me." I put my hand over the receiver and mouthed to him "it's my mother."

"Oh Jesus, Vann. You didn't sound like yourself."

"Mom, it's like one in the morning. Seriously, what's going on?"

"Oh honey, I need you to come home right away. Can you come home tomorrow?"

"Tomorrow? Are you kidding, Mom? I can't just—are you drunk?"

"No! Jesus, Vann." I was mouthing to him that she wanted me to come home. He was telling me to ask her why. She said Jesus like "JEEE-zus". It reminded me of a Baptist minister I heard once on a UCLA trip to Texas.

"Why do need me home, Mom? Is Lisa ok?"

"Yes, she's fine; I'm fine."

"Well, what's going on?"

"I didn't want to tell you over the phone."

"Mom, you're freaking me out. What the fuck is going on."

"Jesus, Vann. Don't say that."

"Fuck?"

"Yes, that!"

"Are going to bitch at me or tell me what's so important that you called me in the middle of the night?

"I wish you wouldn't use those words and that tone—"

"Mom! Seriously!"

"Is your girlfriend with you? Can she come with you?" This one threw me. I mouthed to Dai that she wanted Maru to go with me.

"Damn it, Mom, she's not my girlfriend. She's my wife. We've been together for eight years, married for five of them—like as soon as it became legal. Not girlfriend. Wife. How many times, Mom?" I don't even know what I was arguing about or maybe I was just avoiding the inevitable answer that would in fact draw more unfortunate questions and more inevitable answers I wasn't even sure I knew. Daisuke was rolling his finger like 'get on with it'. I shrugged.

"I don't know how you expect me to keep all this straight. I don't understand—"

"It's not straight. It's the opposite of straight. It's called gay, Mom." But was I really? And what was I fighting about?

"I'm sorry, Vann. I don't want to argue with you right now."

"Me either. Please just tell me what is going on that I need to come home."

"Vann, your father died." There was a long pause as I gathered my thoughts that had been severely jarred by this whole conversation. Daisuke was slapping my arm and asking 'what happened' when he saw me shut down on the spot. I shifted from intense feeling to blankness.

"Honey, I'm sorry. I wanted to tell you in person, but I guess that was a bad idea. Impractical. ... Vann? Are you still there?"

"Yes, Mom. I'm here. No, it—it's ok. I'm just...a...little...unsure what to say." I turned to Dai, eyes wide with bewilderment. He was gesturing vigorously for me to tell him what was going on.

"That's why I wanted Mary there, to comfort you, you know."

"Maru. Her name is Maru." I said flatly.

"Yes, I'm sorry. It's just so—foreign. It's hard to remember."

"It's Japanese, Mom. Mary is not a Japanese name." Daisuke understood what happened and covered his mouth trying not to laugh out loud.

"Oh, Vann. Please don't fuss. Just get here as soon as you can. Both of you are welcome."

"I'll, um, have to make arrangements at work. I work." It was a hot mix of weird feelings. I couldn't sort it out and talk at the same time.

"I know, honey. Just let me know when you can get to the airport. I'll pick you up. I'm so sorry, Vann." I wanted to ask her why, why was she sorry? He was the sorry one. I didn't know him, didn't care about him. But now I would never have the chance. I could never know his secrets—what really happened. I hung up the phone without saying goodbye, without saying anything.

"What was that?" Daisuke burst. My chest constricted and tears overcame my eyelids. "Hey, are you ok?"

"I don't know." He sat up next to me.

"What did she say?" The chocolaty sweetness of his gaze flared with concern.

"My father died." I said matter-of-factly, coldly. He had questions, but he did not ask them. Completely thrown by my own reaction, I just reached out. My arms went to his neck and my lips to his mouth. Hot tears stole into that kiss, a wet stake driving distraction through passion. I blindly reached for him beneath the sheets, still forcing my tongue in his mouth.

He gathered both my wrists in one of his hands and pulled our faces apart. His low-lid stare split me in half. He wasn't about to let me blunt the harshness of those feelings for physical pleasure. He held my eyes and wrists firmly until I stopped fighting for him to just fuck me numb.

Only know. Only don't know.

When he let go, I draped myself across his torso, my face planted in his neck. His arms wrapped around me like a tightly drawn blanket. I melted into wretched weeping.

Chapter 11

The plane took off from LAX and flew me home. Home being Portland, well, Vancouver. Not the cool one in Canada, the one on the north side of the Columbia River. It was early, the first flight leaving at 8:20. My ticket was too expensive at nearly $500, but it didn't matter. I had to go home. Dad was dead.

I stared out the window across the aisle. I couldn't get a window seat because I booked 8 hours before the flight. The night before, I found my way to the shower—too hot and too long. My skin was tight when I emerged. Daisuke reserved my ticket, and I hadn't thought to ask him how he paid for it. I wasn't sure what I had packed. Not much. I had my purse, a backpack and a carry on. I didn't know what I was doing other than going home.

I didn't know my father more than that. Typical hippy couples who thought free love was actually free and didn't require effort, my dad split right after my sister was born. Too heavy I guessed, he wasn't having fun anymore. Lisa was just a few months old; I was still in diapers. If there had been a policy on babies, Mom would have returned us. But she stuck it out and did whatever she could to get by.

I remember seeing my father on summer break when I was 8. I don't remember seeing him before that, but I could have. I was going into second grade. What was there to remember? He came to get us, but it may as well have been a stranger.

Five-year-old energetic inquisitor Lisa was too much for him to handle after a couple of hours and he dropped us off back at our house and drove away while we watched from the driveway. Lisa wanted to play stickers, so we turned on our heels and headed inside. Mom was ready with hugs to comfort us if we were as disappointed as she was. We shrugged it off, pulled out the sticker books and forgot about that weird man who smelled like wet paper and cigarette smoke.

When I started journaling in high school, I wrote about him often. Mostly angry teen angst blabbering. When I got pissed at my mom for not letting me go with a group of friends to see a concert in Portland, I threatened to move in with him. She said "Good luck finding that jackass. And if you do, tell him to pay his child support."

I did find Thomas Townsend. My friend's amateur P.I. mom found him. He was residing in a Shasta County Correctional Facility serving five years for manufacturing and distributing pot in upstate California. Good luck finding that child support. I didn't tell Mom, and especially not Lisa. She had some fantasy about him being off in the Peace Corps in South America and that he was coming back to get us one day and take us to all these exotic places. Knowing she was prone to drama and would be completely crushed to know any hint of the truth, I learned to keep secrets early.

Accepting an offer from UCLA was my biggest secret up to Maru. Mom wanted me to attend Lewis and Clark College, a local liberal arts school. It was small and impossibly close to the one place I wanted to get as far from as I could. Miss Pembroke, my school counselor helped me apply to UCLA that had the technology programs I wanted.

The look of betrayal on my mother's face had a persimmon flavor when I told her.

I moved in with my boyfriend's family for the summer. They were generous and oblivious toward that "sweet little girl," as they called me. They were just happy that their under-achieving, however quite capable son, Chase, was finally dating a respectable girl. The kind that goes to college even though her mom is this crazed control freak. I may have embellished to get out of her house and into theirs, but the sentiment was the same. The Barnes' were sweet, always taking care of me. I tried my best to take nothing more than food from them. My summer job covered my meager expenses and allowed me to save a few thousand bucks for starting school. Chase was not so sweet. He introduced me to my best friend, Reverse Cowgirl. As with any man in his prime, sex with him was fast, furious and frequent. RC was the only way I got mine.

Mrs. Barnes cried when I moved out to go to school. I did too, but not for the same reasons. Mom came to the airport drunk and sobbing. I hugged her anyway and left it all behind.

It wasn't until graduation that I saw my father again. He shocked the hell out of me, a strange man striding up to me, arms outstretched for a hug, on the lawn outside the stadium where I had just walked across the stage and been handed my degree. He said he was so proud of me and how happy he was to see me when it became apparent I had no idea who he was. His receding hair stuck out wildly from his head. Deep lines set into his face that was overly tanned like a field laborer. He wore a mismatched sweat suit and was missing a few teeth. My friends closed in to protect me from whoever this crazy person was.

"Daddy!" Lisa yelled and threw herself into his arms. She had wanted it to be a surprise and it sure was. Having gone out and found him herself living in upstate California two weeks before, she paid for his bus fare to come to the graduation. Ever, the optimist, she thought this was a great idea. Good intentions aside, I would rather have continued imagining him in prison even though his sentence ended years before.

As per her usual, Mom had suggested we all go get a drink, then added 'to celebrate', but that was all she could get out. I reminded her that Lisa was underage, so she suggested Lisa drive. I stood there between these two total fuck ups wondering how you put them together and come up with me. And Lisa, the best of the lot of us. They were pathetic. I did not want to be one of them. I did not want to be one big happy family because there was no such thing. It was too farcical to fake.

We had an awkward lunch while Lisa carried most of the conversation. It was still early, but I couldn't stand it any longer when I excused myself to go celebrate with friends. I tied one on with three or four college buddies, some not even celebrating graduation yet. It didn't matter. I was going to get fucked and fucked up before the night was over. I danced and slammed Modern English cocktails until my feet and my head pounded in rhythm. At 3-something a.m., I presented myself at my on-again-off again boyfriend Dave's apartment and slammed him too.

It was an all-weekend drunken fuck fest. Anything to avoid feeling real. I wanted to displace the reality that I was a purebred failure and have a fine time in the process. I still wanted to turn on my heel and forget that strange man who still smelled like cigarette smoke and wet paper.

Two years later, Maru had been the only one waiting to celebrate with me when I picked up my Masters. Lisa had married and was too pregnant to fly. She did not invite Dad as a surprise that time either. I forget my mother's excuse, but I didn't care as long as Maru was there. And she was, always.

As our early months stretched into years, she became my whole family. My mother when I needed consoling, my father when I needed stability, my sister when I needed someone to talk to, my brother when I needed a buddy to knock around with.

I was thinking about what an awesome burden I had lain on her when the plane landed in Portland with a thump and jerk. The whooshing sound of the reverse thrusters drowned out everything but the memory of his wide face coming at me on the lawn. I think if I had reacted differently, maybe I could have known him. Like he was reaching out then, but I had already let go. If I had taken a stab at being honest instead of evasive, maybe I wouldn't be flying home to bury a man I met only twice and knew only by name and shitty smell.

I thought of Daisuke and checked my phone for missed calls I knew wouldn't be there. He was strangely quiet on the way to the airport. So was I. I guess there's nothing to say in times like those, but I couldn't help noticing the finality in our final embrace outside the car, Maru's car. Dad, Daisuke, Maru—all these worlds crashed together right there on the yellow lines. I felt more alone, more abandoned. A dumped orphan.

Dai wasn't saying goodbye, like 'this is it' goodbye. But he was saying he knew I would be different when I came home. Losing a parent changes you in a harsh and fundamental way. Losing one like I did, with no way to go back, no way to know, no way to piece together anything but disappointment, was nasty and cruel.

I thought I wouldn't really care when Dad died. He wasn't anyone to me. But when it actually happened, I found myself wishing I could go back to that graduation and slap the shit out of myself. Wake up! You don't get any other chances, I would yell at my own face. You never see him again!

No chance to get it out, to try to understand him, to try to understand myself. The finality was chilling. I was not prepared, nor could I have been. I stood at the edge of an endless lake looking at the icy surface for answers. My own reflection stared back at me, looking for answers. The chasm of isolation opened up and swallowed me whole.

Chapter 12

I was angry, briefly, that Mom hadn't come to pick me up at the airport. Then I remembered I never called her back and she didn't know I was home. I flagged a cabbie to take me across the river to her modest bungalow on Evergreen Blvd.

I'm not sure how I thought it was going to play out. Besides the whole dead Dad thing, I was about to show up without Maru and absolutely no aspiration to explain. What was I supposed to say? Yeah, so I got left in the night and started sleeping with her brother like comfort food? But it's all good because I'm learning so much about myself. Should I have just said I was seeing someone else and not mention that they were actually related? Maybe I was hoping Mom would be drunk and Lisa would be so depressed they wouldn't notice.

In any case, I had not formulated a plot until, in fact, I dragged my carryon, purse and backpack up the driveway. I rapid-fired a couple of scenarios: wholly evading the topic, simply lying and/or bending the truth in such a way that I didn't have to flat out say how completely fucked up I was—just like she and Dad had been. Pulling out the key to her house, I decided that I did not want to be in the closet ever again. I didn't want to hide or lie to try to make someone else feel comfortable or avoid answering for the ugliness that had spiraled into my existence. It's too complicated and cheap to try to keep up with whatever fabrication I might spin. If these past few weeks with Daisuke had meant anything to me at all, I would lay it bare. I had been naïve; I had no excuses for my behavior. All shame and embarrassment aside, I couldn't go in there all holier-than-thou, judge these people and pretend like I was flawless. I had never been flawless and never would be. I had seen so many new facets about myself and how I had lived an egotistical life, I would not betray them now. I was Vann Townsend: blissfully self-centered, until very recently at least. Now I was more akin to Vann Townsend: bitter realist.

I let myself in and stood in the front foyer for a long moment, listening, breathing, bracing.

"Hello?" Lisa called from the kitchen.

"It's me, Lisa." I forced myself forward. She sprang from the chair and threw her arms around me and my bags. She pinned my arms under her fearful embrace. I let the purse and backpack slip to the floor so I could get an arm around her.

"I am so glad you're here," she whispered in my ear.

"Me too, babe." I lied. She was crying, and probably had been since last night. We stood like that until my shoulder burned and let go. "Where's Mom?"

"She went to the store."

"The liquor store?"

"Most likely." Lisa shook her head.

"Good. I hope she brings back something besides vodka or gin." Lisa's face was cross. "What? She's going to drink anyway."

"You don't have to encourage her."

"Who said anything about encouraging her? I guess I'm at a place where I'm understanding her and saying, 'I'll have what she's having.'"

"Are you a drunk now?"

"Lisa, it's eleven o'clock in the morning. I won't be drunk until at least noon." I waited a second for her to catch on.

"That's not funny, Vann. She has a real problem."

"That's sweet, really, Lisa. But do you think ragging her about it is going to help?"

"What about you, though?"

"What about me? I've always blunted fucked up feelings with alcohol." I said with a heavy exhale. Honesty can be so relieving and wickedly confusing at the same time. "And sex, apparently." I admitted.

"What are you talking about?"

"I'm just talking. I don't want to bullshit anymore. I'm done with it."

"Since when?"

"Oh, very recently..." I trailed off into old patterns of evading discomfort. She narrowed her eyes and tried to figure out this new character wearing her sister's face.

"Where is your wife?" she asked slowly.

"So yeah, that's about when 'very recently' started."

"What happened, Vann?" She was strained and mad that something clearly was wrong, and I hadn't talked to her about it.

"Where are your kids? Where's Mike?"

"He has the kids at home. Don't ignore my question."

"No, Lisa. I wasn't...it's just kind of a long story. I was hoping to talk to you and Mom at the same time."

"No, you're going to tell me now. I know you—"

"Knew me," I corrected her. "I'm not the same person anymore, babe."

"Well, Maru's not here. And you're acting weird, so I'm guessing nothing good happened."

"No, it's been good. In a break-a-mirror-with-your-face-so-you-can-see-yourself kind of way." I sat at the kitchen table and smoothed my fly-aways back into my ponytail. "She left me."

"What? What happened? You guys have been together like...forever."

"Yeah well, forever doesn't last forever anymore, Lis."

"Was it someone else? Did she just get done with you, what?" My eyebrows twisted with my frown.

"That's the real bitch. I don't know. She literally walked away. Left her whole life behind like a tornado in a trailer park. Her car, her stuff, her wallet, me, all of it."

"Where did she go with all that nothing?"

"I don't know. I seriously don't know, babe."

"What do you mean, Vann. That's crazy." I looked up at her. She reached across the table for my hand.

"She up and left in the night. I nearly filed a missing person's report until I talked her brother. Which is a whole other story."

"You don't know why she left?"

"I don't know where she went, where she is, how she got there, why she left, why she left like she did, if she's coming back, nothing. I've never known so little about someone I love so much. Nothing, I know nothing."

"You know you love her."

"Do I? I don't know."

"I do. I know you love her. I can see it on you. And sometimes it takes letting her go to really know her."

"That's bullshit, Lisa. I'm not in the mood."

"You are being such a bitch. What is it with you?"

"I think we're both under some stress. I really didn't need Dad to die right now."

"So sorry it didn't fit your schedule." She was snarky. It was time to show my hand.

"I'm fucking her brother." Her eyes bulged and mouth fell open. "I'm not proud—"

"You're what?"

"I said I'm not proud of it. It wasn't intentional—"

"Wait, what? You can't say it wasn't intentional if you're fuck-ing her brother. That implies present tense, like multiple, like for real."

"Oh, it's very real."

"Oh my god. Who are you?"

"I didn't know how to tell you. I didn't know if you'd understand."

"Well, that's one way to tell me. And no, I don't understand, V."

"I don't really either. He…he…comforts me," I got out.

"I'm sure he does 'comfort' you. What in the holy hell is going on with you?"

"That's a fair question. I guess I sort of got dumped upside down when Maru left and freaked out."

"Freaked out? Freaked out, Vann? Freaking out is getting depressed, freaking out is drinking too much—"

"Oh, I did that too."

"Freaking out is not fucking your wife's b-r-o-t-h-e-r," she said so deliberately it stung. "That's in a whole other category. Does she know?"

"No idea. Neither of us have heard from her since she disappeared."

"Disappeared? How long ago was that?"

"Like three months."

"Three months! Oh my god, Vann. You can't call me in three months and tell me shit like this." I laughed a little. "What is so funny?"

"It's funny to hear you cussing."

"You're freaking me out. And pissing me off. Good god, I hope Mom brings home some very red wine."

"I told you..."

"No, you didn't tell me. You didn't tell me any of this? It's like saying, 'oh, by the way, Mike and I had another baby last year'."

"Is that three now?"

"We didn't have a baby! I'm just saying. Jesus, Vann!"

"Well, now you sound like Mom. Jesus this, Jesus that."

"Go fuck yourself. We aren't like that. At least I thought we weren't like those people that just don't talk."

"I said I didn't know how to tell you. And frankly I'm a little embarrassed but at the same time in total awe of this whole sequence in my shit show."

"I can't believe what you're telling me right now. Are you not gay?"

"Hell, babe, I don't know. It's more...fluid than that." I searched for the word.

"Fluid like when a man cums all over you?"

"Gross, no. It's not like that. I'm mean my own sexual preference can't just be nailed down to one label as 'gay' or 'straight'."

"You're just a slut then, I guess."

"Hey, that's not fair. Slut has nothing to do with the gender of who I'm sleeping with. You know more than anyone that my relationship with Maru was a surprise to me."

"Well, the end of it is pretty surprising too. What's going to happen when she comes home?"

"That's just it. We don't know. We talk about it all the time. But it's kind of ugly any way you look at it. I imagine it won't go much better than this very conversation."

"We? We who? I don't even know his name."

"Daisuke."

“What?”

“Die-soo-kee,” I pronounced phonetically.

“What kind of name is that?”

“Japanese, Lisa. You know Maru is Japanese. So is he.”

“Say it again.” I did. “Maru was hard enough to get used to. This is messed up.”

“It’s been really…liberating, actually. I don’t think I ever knew myself, or Maru, as well as I do now. It’s opening all these new ways of seeing.”

“And fucking, apparently.”

“And fucking, yes.”

“I wasn’t serious. Gross.” I could see her thinking.

“It’s taken a little…mmm…getting used to.”

“I guess so. It’s been what, almost ten years?”

“Eight.”

“That’s messed up. Seriously, what are you going to do?”

“Well, I don’t really know that she’s ever coming, like, home. To me. But I guess that’s something I’ll find out when and if it ever happens.”

“Are you going to be like, ‘so sorry, I didn’t mean to sleep with your brother, several times?’”

“Hey, you’re supposed to be on my side. She left me. I thought she was dead. That’s a really fucked up thing to do to someone you love. And even if she never loved me, that’s a fucked-up thing to do to someone who loves you.

“Ok, true.”

“Maybe sleeping with her brother was a little mean, but she gave up her rights to all that when she went off.”

“A little mean? That’s the understatement of the century, don’t you think?”

“Don’t you think I know it would hurt her?”

“Did you do it to get back at her?”

“No! Not at all. It wasn’t like that.”

"How was it, then?"

"Lisa, I fell apart after she left. I mean like really bad."

"Because you didn't call your sister."

"You don't want to hear about my shit. You have a life and a family, and it doesn't include your Lesbo older sister's complications."

"Ouch. That's harsh."

"I'm serious. I was so FUBAR I didn't know up from down for a few days."

"A few days? It's been a few months."

"I guess I was hoping she would come back, and it would blow over. After a couple of months, I had to start making decisions about our stuff, her stuff. I can't really afford our lifestyle on my salary alone."

"Who knew a cook made so much money?"

"Now you're showing your ignorance. She makes more whittling fish than your husband does, dumbass. It's an art."

"Oh, ok. An art. Mike makes enough to support us with his job in construction."

"I'm sure he does, honey, but you don't live in downtown L.A."

"Excu-use me. I didn't realize your life was so hard."

"See, that's what I'm talking about."

"What?"

"Right there. You have all your shit and your life. And for me it was just us. We had good jobs, plenty of money. We didn't struggle. Your kids and stay-home mom status are not my fault."

"I wasn't blaming you."

"No, you're just saying I have it so easy because I don't have 2.5 kids, a mortgage and all that."

"But that's true."

"Those are the choices you made about your life. Not me. I chose something else that involved a different lifestyle."

"I thought you didn't like it when people called it a 'lifestyle'."

"Lisa. Focus! I'm not trying to argue with you. I'm just saying I didn't want to talk to you about it because you have plenty of your own problems up here."

"You didn't want to talk to me about it because you're a pussy." My eyes bulged this time. "That's so you, Vann. Get drunk and fuck someone. But don't dare face your own problems." She said it so matter-of-factly, I was instantly incensed. "It's the same thing every time, isn't it? Did you think I didn't know?"

"I guess I don't care if you know how I cope with my shit."

"That's not coping, fucktard. It's avoiding having to deal with pain."

"Did you call me a 'fucktard?'"

"Yes, I did. Because you're fucking retarded."

"Fucktard? Really. I know what it means, you little shit."

"Well, there you go. Now that's it's getting real, you're going in to shut-down mode. Are you looking for Mom to come in from the liquor store so you can numb all this out already?"

"Damn right, I am."

"Why is it so hard for you to just deal with yourself?"

"I have been dealing with myself. Who do you think you are?"

"Who do you think you are?"

"I'm your sister. I'm your fucking sister. And I just told you I got my heart wrenched out of my chest and you're stomping on it."

"Am I? Or is that what you're telling yourself so you don't have to admit you're just as much a fuck up as the rest of us?"

"What, do you want me to say I'm a fuck up? I'm a fucking fuck up, Lisa! There you go." I completely exploded. "I ran off my wife and fucked the holy shit out of her brother. And I liked it—fucking loved it. We came at the same time! Who does that? And because I'm such a fuck up, I did it again. And I don't feel bad. In fact, I'm thinking about fucking him right now! About how I'd rather be screwing my brains out than here with you and Mom trying to figure out what to do with our fucking father. And I don't know what's coming next, goddamned it! Where the fuck is Mom already?" I pounded the table panting.

"Feel better?" She smiled with satisfaction. The stab of poignancy is never a relief. She always had a way of getting under my skin—a hallmark usually reserved for the older sibling.

"You're right," I cut my eyes at her. "Fuck you for that."

"You're welcome."

"I'm not thanking you."

"You're still welcome."

"I'm not kidding, that was too far."

"Nah. You handled it like a champ. You needed to pull that cactus out of your ass."

"You're unbelievable. I can tell you get enjoyment from this."

"It's true, I do. But it's a small consolation in my stay-at-home mom existence."

"Seriously, fuck you."

"Can we move on?"

"Don't do that to me again; it fucking hurts." She leaned across the table and stared me down.

"It's supposed to. It's called dealing with your issues. It's this new health craze. And do you have any other adjective in your vocabulary? Really?"

"Fuck fuck fuck, fucking fuck."

"It's your favorite."

"I can't believe you're giving me a fucking lecture."

"Apparently, I'm the one that needs a fucking lecture. You're the one with all the good sex. I haven't had an orgasm in like, two or three years." She laughed.

"God, that must suck." I laughed with her. It felt good, old-sisters good.

"What sucks is hearing about your five and six orgasms at a time. I seriously don't think I've had that many total." I put my arm around her and pulled her into a hug.

"I'm not going to tell you how to cum, Lisa. It's weird."

"Not, me. Work on Mike. He has one every time."

"Oh, that's just awful. I don't even want to think about it." She hugged me back and we hung in the moment. She finally pulled away and looked at me curiously.

"What's he look like?"

"Her. He looks just like her. He smells like her, he even feels like her. I mean, I swear if I close my eyes, it's her hands on me."

"Whoa. That's messed up. Sounds like a surrogate. Do you have a picture?"

"Surrogate?" I asked and pulled up photos on my phone.

"Yeah, it's like you're projecting your want for her on him."

"No, he's totally different." I defended.

"Is he? You just told me how he was just like her."

"But he's different, too. I mean physically, they're like clones. Except for the one thing. But he talks to me differently. And I talk to him differently too. I can tell him anything, anything." She scrolled through the photos.

"Jesus, he does look like her. But hotter."

"Maybe because you're attracted to men." I gave her a look. "But our relationship is completely something else on its own." She landed on a photo he had taken with my phone. It was from our bare shoulders up. I was asleep on his chest, my face planted in his neck. He smiled softly. The afterglow seeped out of the phone.

"You look happy in these photos. Like, really happy. So does he. Do you love him?" That familiar squeeze in my chest made my eyes water.

"I think I do."

"You think you do?"

"I mean, I haven't thought about it until just now."

"So, you love him?" I looked away.

"Doesn't that depend on your definition of love?"

"What does it mean to you?"

"What are you, a psychologist?"

"It was my major in college."

"You never graduated, psycho."

"Oh shit, I forgot," she said sarcastically.

"I don't know what love means to me. I know I'd rather be with him than without him. I know I've never experienced life so completely, so openly and honestly with him. Does that mean I love him?"

"That's up to you, isn't it?"

"Right, Dr. Powers." My turn with sarcasm. She rolled her eyes.

"Do you still love your wife? I'm assuming you're still married."

"Yes, I love her," I shot back. "I can't not love her. It's part of my DNA now. I miss her every day; I miss us; I miss the way we used to be."

"That's probably it, really. You miss the way your life used to be before you knew what it was like to hurt in such fundamental way."

"Yeah, that sounds about right, actually. I hate that you're right, but you are."

"So, Vann Xandria Townsend. How does this all end up?" I didn't have a middle name. It was replaced with an 'X' when one was required, so we had long ago made up a middle name that only Lisa used.

"No idea. Having expectations seems terrifying and impractical right now."

"See, that's real stuff."

"Are we having a breakthrough here, Dr. Powers?"

"I believe we are Miss Townsend."

"It's still Mrs." I corrected sharply.

"Right-o, sorry. Hey, what would your name be if you married Dikesee?"

"It's Daisuke, and we're not getting married. You couldn't pronounce it anyway."

"Touché."

"I'm still married. I still love my wife. And, strangely, I also love her brother."

"This is like some Homer, incest epic. Do you think you could have them both?"

"Oh god, I don't want to think about it. I don't think I could handle them both."

"I wasn't serious, Vann. That's messed up that you would think I was serious."

"I'll give you that."

"I guess the question is: which of them do you want?"

"I don't think that's the question. I don't even know if I'll have a chance at getting Maru back. I may have mentioned she left me like a bad party, and I don't know anything about where she is or why..."

"You know she's going to be really, really...really hurt, right?" I nodded.

"There's no scenario where this ends well."

"So, which will it be?"

"I can't—I can't choose. That's so unfair. Nothing about this whole jacked up situation is fair."

"Hey, are you on the pill or something?"

“No, why?”

“Uh, hello. You’re the one who just reminded me why I never finished college. Unprotected straight sex has…consequences.”

“I guess I didn’t think about it. I didn’t have a period for two months after she left. He said it was probably stress.”

“He said? How would he know.”

“He’s a surgeon. Well, almost hand surgeon.”

“Almost a hand surgeon?”

“He’s finishing up his residential.”

“Wow, a doctor, too. Can it get any easier for you?”

“Ok, tell me what about this sounds easy.”

“Right again. So, you don’t think you could be pregnant?”

“Stop wishing hateful things on me.”

“Children aren’t hateful things, Vann.”

“They are when you have to explain to your wife she has a son and a nephew” I faked a sunny tone.

“Could be sticky, yes. But why don’t you use protection?”

“Well, shit. I guess I didn’t think about it. I’m not pregnant though.”

“You say that…”

“I know.” I was pretty sure I knew, at least. In any case, I made a mental note to put in a call to my gynecologist.

“Wouldn’t that be totally crazy.”

“Way beyond that. I told you I didn’t need Dad to die right now.”

“When would have been a good time for it to fit in your schedule?”

“Seriously, where is Mom?”

“I’ll send her a text and tell her you’re home.”

“She texts now?”

“You really should come home more than every other year, V.” I consented with a nod and checked the door again.

"Lisa what happened? To Dad? What happened?"

"Well, let's see, when was the last time you saw him."

"You know when it was. It was your 'surprise', remember?"

"You never saw him after your graduation?"

"Undergrad. No one was at my graduate graduation, except Maru."

"You know I couldn't be there."

"What's your point?"

"I was seven months pregnant!"

"No, no. About not seeing Dad since then."

Before she could answer my question like a hot poker in my throat, the front door opened. I heard the crinkling and clinking of bags making their way toward us. Mom was home.

Chapter 13

"Lisa!" My mom called from the hallway. "Have you heard from your sister yet? She never called me back; I don't even know if she's coming. This is just like her." I gave Lisa a look to make sure she didn't interrupt. "Forget about my family," Mom said mocking my voice. "I have a life in L.A." She rounded the corner into the kitchen.

"Hey Mom." I tried to look hurt but burst out laughing instead. She flushed. "Sorry I forgot to call you back last night." I got too much pleasure from watching her squirm. She laid the bags on the table with a humph and tried to adjust herself into Mother mode.

"She was busy," Lisa said. Mom shot her a nasty look.

"Well, I'm glad you're here, now." She said straightening her collar.

"Are you?" I asked.

"Yes, honey." She feigned a one-armed hug. "I'm so sorry to have to tell you about your father like that on the phone."

"No really, it's fine. Lisa was just reminding me that I needed to reconnect at home." She smiled.

"Well, you do." She pulled a box of wine from the bag. "You only come every couple of years, and you miss all the family stuff."

"Ok, first, I acknowledge I'm not the perfect sister or daughter. Second, I didn't realize we were ever anything like people who do 'family stuff.' We're barely related. And third, if the two of you are going to beat me up the whole time, I'll go stay someplace else."

"Vann, don't be so offended. I just want you around more—"

"And fourth, you've only come to visit me once. For my graduation. Ten, almost 11 years ago."

"Let's don't do this," Lisa started in. "Just stop now. Every time we get together..." she strained to reel herself in. "Let's just focus on Dad."

"I'm all for that. You were just about to tell me what happened to him when you pointed out I hadn't seen him since, oh, the last time you visited me, Mom." I gave her a parting shot.

"Seriously, V?" Lisa pressed her fingers to her temples. "Let's just get through this. Mom, it's not even noon. Put the glasses away."

"I just thought—I was trying to be helpful."

"You were just trying to find an excuse to get drunk before lunch," I said.

"Oh, that's rich—" she stopped short, but I knew what she meant. "Where's your gir—wife?"

"Aw Mom." I said smiling and patting the back of her hand. "Thanks for trying to remember we are legally married. I'm touched." Lisa cleared her throat.

"Vann was just telling me why Maru wasn't able to come..." They both looked at me waiting for me to spit it out. My turn to squirm. I stalled so I could think of something quick, then exhaled all the way out.

"She left me, Mom."

"What?"

"And?" Lisa goaded.

"Well...it's been a little crazy in the Townsend house since then."

"A little crazy?" Lisa coughed.

"Ok, it's been...really...psychotically delirious, actually." She sat down as I told her the whole story, forging a look of absolute shock on her face. I couldn't tell if she was happy, sad, sorry, ecstatic or numb. She listened to Lisa and me go back and forth about the whole affair, eyeing the paper bag occasionally and leaning further and further over the table with every sordid detail until her sizable girth pushed it an inch across the floor.

"Well. That's quite a...situation." She finally got out. I arched my eyebrows and crossed my arms, completely undone. From one end to the other, I was pinned open like an insect for dissection. "And now this," she added.

"Yeah. Just what I needed."

"It's too bad your life was perfect, sis. See how much fun you were missing all this time." I gave her a wounded look.

"So, surprise, Mom. I'm just as much a fuck up as any of us."

"Is that what you think? That we're screw ups?"

"That's not exactly what I said."

"Look around, Vann. The whole world is full of 'em! Welcome to the club, little girl." And with that, she went straight for Hawkeye vodka—the hangover guarantee. I fished in the bag then pushed it away, disgusted.

"Anybody ready to move on?" Lisa asked.

"Would someone please just tell me how Dad died?"

"Vann, told me she hadn't seen him since we all came to her graduation?"

"Really? That's too bad."

"Why do you two pretend like he wasn't a total loser? Like he didn't leave you when things got real, Mom. And that he was never the hero you fantasized about, Lisa?"

"Wow, she doesn't know, does she?" Lisa said to Mom.

"Know what? That he was an addict and a felon and a terrible father?"

"Guess not," Mom said to Lisa.

"You missed a lot."

"Doesn't seem like I could have missed much. And stop being so cryptic. Why won't you just tell me how he fucking died?"

"Well, they said he had a stroke."

"Finally, ok. The guy dies of a stroke at 55?"

"Fifty-four. Our father was 54."

"Whatever. Who is they? Where was he and where is he now. How do we get this over with?"

"They were the people from the Zen center. One of the practice leaders called yesterday and told us about the stroke."

"Zen center? What was he doing there?"

"That's what I've been trying to tell you. He's been a resident at the Tassajara Zen Center for almost 12 years now."

"Wait, what?"

"So apparently the Zen center has this prison outreach program. Their practice leaders visit prisoners offering support and guidance for inmates interested in meditation and Buddhism. Dad started going to their meditation and yoga classes while he was in prison at San Quentin."

"So, you knew he had been in prison?"

"You didn't?"

"No, I knew. I found out before I left home for UCLA. I just didn't want to tell you because you had this romanticized ideal of our father and I didn't want ruin it for you."

"I don't think I had any ideal about Dad. I just loved him no matter what he did." Mom nodded and patted Lisa's hand.

"I guess I'm just a heartless bitch for my huge expectations of him, like showing up or paying child support or not breaking the law."

"Always playing the victim." Lisa said and rolled her eyes.

"We were all victims of his absence, of how he lived his life—without us, without responsibility for any of his actions."

"He served his time for his actions, Vann," Lisa said, pleading. "And when he really wanted to start over and be a better man as well as a better father, I was willing to forgive him everything else."

"So, you two have been in contact all these years?

"Off and on, yes. We wrote letters mostly, but he came to visit a few times too."

"Why did you never tell me about all this?"

"He asked me not to. Said it would be better for you if you if he stayed out of the picture until you were ready."

"That sounds like bullshit to me. Like he just took the low-hanging fruit, Lisa."

"You're saying I made it too easy for him? Maybe I just wanted a father and didn't demand a perfect father."

"Well, I guess I just suck, then."

"You see what you're doing? You're deflecting your failures with self-depreciation."

"I thought we already went through this. Can you just please tell me what you know about our current situation?" She rolled her eyes again; she knew how much I hated the childish gesture.

She told me about how after he got out of prison, about two years before my graduation, he practiced and volunteered at the San Francisco Zen Center. Somewhere in there, he decided to become a resident at their Zen training monastery living like a monk. She had gone to visit him there once and said he seemed really happy—at peace.

"Good for him, but what about all the people he'd hurt?" I thought but didn't say.

She said he took refuge, the Buddhist version of getting saved without the whole deity thing. He took the precepts, which were like the Ten Commandments, but there were 11 and they were vows. He'd been training and teaching at the Zen Mountain Zen Center for the past eight years.

One of the resident practice leaders found him in his dorm room. He was incoherent, throwing up and unable to get off the floor. She called an ambulance, but he died on the way to the hospital.

"Did they try to revive him?" I asked.

"I don't think so," Mom said. "I think he had a DNR order or something like that."

"So, wow, he just turned his life into something else entirely?"

"Yeah, he did," Lisa said. "It's sad you missed it. Mike, the kids and I have some pretty good memories of him."

"I still don't see why he wouldn't have contacted me if he was so changed."

"He said he didn't want to be an intrusion. But really, Vann, would you have tried to contact you? You're pretty hard to live up to."

"What's that supposed to mean?"

"It means your expectations are impossible. Sure, you're all humble now, but don't tell me you didn't think you were better than us before your love triangle tangle."

"Ok, girls." Mom interrupted. "That's enough. You need to support each other right now."

"What about you?" I asked, the devil's advocate. "You can't support us right now."

"This isn't my battle, honey. You're the ones that have to work through all this."

"Being married to him had no effect on you? You're not sad that he's gone?"

"I'm mostly sad for my girls having to deal with losing a parent so early in life."

"Yeah, Vann. We have some stuff to work out. Let's just focus on that right now."

"That's what I've been trying to do. Just get this over with."

"I don't think it's going to be that easy for us."

"Don't we just plan a funeral and put him in the ground." Lisa scoffed.

"He's Buddhist, Vann. You don't bury a Buddhist."

"Oh, right. We're supposed to have him cremated?"

"Actually, he was very detailed with his final wishes," Lisa said. I heard apprehension in her voice and wondered what was coming.

"Like what?"

"He wants a traditional Buddhist funeral, and he wants us both to be there."

"They're not sending him up here?"

"No, he's at Tassajara; they're waiting for us to get there."

"What's the funeral supposed to be like? And what are we supposed to do?"

"I don't know all the details, just that they keep the body undisturbed for three days before cremation. We're supposed to be there by Thursday."

"Keep the body undisturbed? Sounds weird."

"The center director didn't say much other than the family should come as soon as possible because they don't embalm. She said they would give us an orientation when we arrived."

"Orientation? This is...a lot to take in."

"I know, right. I was completely shocked when I got the call. My mind was all over the place. But at the same time, she seemed so comforting to me."

"So, what now?"

"Now we go to Tassajara."

"How are we going to get a flight today?"

"You can drive," Mom said.

"Yeah, we can drive down," Lisa said.

"Really? That's like a seven-, eight-hour drive from here."

"It's twelve to Tassajara. That's not too bad. Besides, we're going to need a car when we get there. One with four-wheel drive apparently."

"Why's that?"

"Tassajara is at the end of a long, rough road on top of a mountain."

"How fitting. Sounds just like how Dad lived...and then died."

Chapter 14

Curiosity kept guilt from hollowing me out. There was much I didn't know about Timothy Townsend's second act. Would I have liked him? What would he have thought about Maru? I pictured them in practice robes, drinking hot tea together and chuckling at how I say "fuck" a lot.

I simultaneously needled myself for writing him off and cursed him for not reaching out to me. None of it was fair. Around and around, I blamed him then felt responsible for being judgmental and unapproachable. I had made up my mind very early that I wouldn't end up like him. And still, I was jarred and ashamed that I had been the one to disown the family.

Lisa and I made plans to drive to San Francisco and stay the night, then finish the trip in the morning. We borrowed Mike's work truck which gulped gas like my mom chugged cheap liquor. It was the only thing that would take us the final leg up the mountain. The truck was manual. I appreciated Daisuke's insistence that I learn how to drive Maru's stick. Mike didn't object to taking the minivan to his job site but looked truly terrified about being left alone with the girls for five days. Keeping them was Mom's only contribution other than refilling drinks.

Lisa and I knitted our threadbare sisterhood as we prepared for the journey. We usually worked well together when we weren't going for each other's throats. We didn't know what to expect or how to dress. I brought little with me. The black dress that would have worked for a typical funeral but felt off for anything Buddhist. Mike found us a sleep cheap in Walnut Creek, but we'd have to leave in half an hour to get there by 10:00 PM. We had no time to formulate complete thoughts.

Everything moved quickly, and in slow motion at the same time. My head was on overload with Maru, Daisuke and Dad colliding, each asking me to face hard truths. Lisa could tell I was in turmoil and laid off the psychoanalyst routine. With the route to our hotel telling me to turn left from the driveway, we shoved off.

Lisa offered to drive first. I'd been up since 5 AM and didn't object. Daisuke would be on shift at the hospital. I sent him a message anyway.

Going to Tassajara Zen Center. Long story, but Dad changed, and I missed it. Wish I could talk to you about this. Be home in 5 days.

I sent Kate a text about bereavement leave. She offered to feed Grover and Emi, for which I was grateful since I had forgotten about them in my haste. I felt relieved and drowsy when I leaned the seat back and it all faded away.

The grating scrape of metal on metal woke me. Lisa fueled up at some remote gas station in Roseburg. I peeled myself from the passenger's seat and stretched.

"Do you want anything?" I asked her.

"Get me a coffee and maybe some of those little..."

"Zebra cakes?"

"Yeah. Thanks."

"They're your favorite." I bought some equally horrible gas station food and a 60 oz bucket of Coke on the rocks. I juggled the junk out to the truck.

"Here's to spoiling our dinner," I laughed, handing over the stash.

"No kidding." She took a long pull on the coffee. "We can stop in Redding for dinner."

"How far is it?"

"Few more hours, or so."

"Do you want me to drive?"

"I will at Redding," she said, climbing back in the oversized truck. "I hate driving at night, especially in a big city."

"Walnut Ridge isn't any bigger than Vancouver."

"I promise you don't want me to drive through there."

"Fair enough." I snapped my seatbelt together. I thought I might need a crane to lower my drink into the cup holder without spilling it and opted to drink some off the top.

"So do you know anything about these Buddhist customs," she asked as we exited onto the freeway.

"Not really."

"I thought being married to someone Japanese, you might have some ideas about what we're getting into."

"Maru isn't a practicing Buddhist. I don't even know her parents. They may be."

"What about your boyfriend?" she teased. I blushed but didn't want to.

"He's not my boyfriend. And he's not very Buddhist either. Really, he's mostly like any other American guy. He was still young when they came here so he picked up more on this culture than his own."

"You've never met their parents?"

"Oh, hell no. Maru didn't speak to them, and Daisuke and I are unofficial."

"How funny. You're back in the closet."

"I am not," I shot. "We're just not telling anyone right now."

"How is that not in the closet?"

"For starters, I'm not divorced yet. And then there's the whole brother/sister thing. Ok, maybe you're right."

"You think maybe?"

"Do you always have to be right?"

"Only when I am."

"That's not an answer."

"You know, I've missed you."

"Me too. We used to have some good times when we were kids."

"When was the last time we got to do something together with just the two of us?"

"Before you had the kids, I guess. When I took you shopping on Santa Monica."

"Oh god, I was so exhausted after just a couple of hours of that mess."

"You were going to college. I wanted you to look glamorous."

"It apparently worked. I wore that sundress with the little white belt on my first date with Mike."

"The one with that went with the yellow sandals?"

"Yeah, that one."

"You looked totally hot in that!"

"Yeah, thanks. Too hot apparently..."

"Apparently."

"We did used to have fun running around Vancouver as kids, didn't we? At least until you were like what, 15 or 16?"

"Sixteen."

""Why, what happened."

"That's when I found Dad. Do you remember my friend Jake?"

"Yeah."

"His mom was like this wanna-be private investigator. She did some digging for me and found him at San Quentin."

"Is that how you found out? Did you go see him?"

"No. I had no desire. I was pissed at Mom about something and told her I was going to find him and go live with him. I felt stupid and embarrassed. I guess it was then that I was ready to get out of Vancouver for good. Based on Dad's track record, I just thought that would be the usual for him, in and out of jail, in and out of our lives."

"I'm not saying he wasn't like that, Vann. But he had really come around after that. It's too bad how this all played out."

"I know, Lisa. I don't think any of us got everything right, especially not me. But after what I've been going through, I can honestly tell you the 'what ifs' don't help. You just take up again with whatever's left."

"You know, I thought you left because of me for the longest time."

"Why would you think something like that?"

"I don't know. I thought, why would you take off and leave me if I hadn't made you mad."

"Oh, Lisa. I'm so sorry. It had nothing to do with you."

"Yes, it did. Maybe not directly, but with you gone, Mom just got worse and worse, blaming everything on you and taking it out on me."

"I didn't know Lisa, you have to believe me. Why didn't you tell me? I maybe could have—"

"Could have what? Come home and really pissed her off? Gotten me in real trouble for squealing? Were you going to come back from UCLA and save me?"

"I don't know. I would have done something. What happened?"

"Nothing. Nothing at all."

"Tell me Lisa. I want to know."

"That is what happened. She ignored me completely most of the time when she wasn't drunk and crying. Nothing I did ever impressed her or made her happy. It was like being an indentured servant."

"Why did you stay? I mean why didn't you get out of there?"

"Where was I going to go? I didn't have any rich boyfriends to shack up with or the grades to go out of state like you did. I couldn't even get into Lewis & Clark."

"I thought you were just getting your prerequisites at community college. You were supposed to go on to a full university, remember?"

"Oh, I remember. I remember thinking you were delusional, that I wasn't cut out for that. Then I met Mike in my composition class. If it wasn't him, it would have been any other guy that paid attention to me."

"You got pregnant on purpose?" I covered my mouth with both hands.

"Mike was my UCLA, Vann. Don't you get it? He was my way out."

"Oh, that's so sad. Did you ever love him?"

"Sure I did. I still do. He's a great man; he supports us and is a loving father."

"But what. Why does this sound like some commercial?"

"I always wanted what you had. Always."

"What I had? We had the same life, Lisa. Why couldn't you have done all the things I did?"

"Vann, you can be so stupid."

"What? How am I so stupid?"

"You were always the hot one, got whatever you wanted from people. You were popular and smart. And never afraid of anything. Completely fearless."

"Is that what you thought? I was afraid of everything. I was afraid I would fail in college, I would go broke and have to come home. There were so many times I nearly gave in. I had to fight for everything."

"Yeah, you were always the fighter. I'm the sweet one, remember. Sweet doesn't get you anything but knocked up."

"That's such bullshit, Lisa. You could have done anything you wanted."

"You knew. I didn't. I was desperate to get away from Mom's drama network."

"How did I never know this? Why didn't we ever talk about this?"

"Because you don't talk about this stuff, Vann. It's ugly and you don't want to know."

"I'm your sister. I want to know. I would have helped you in any way I could."

"You know the real kicker? Here's my sister who could have really any guy she wanted on personality alone, much less your looks. And you call me up and tell me you're with a woman. You're in love and getting married?"

"What's wrong with that? I thought you were ok with it."

"Sure, I was. I love you. I want you to be happy."

"So, what's the kicker?"

"It's stupid," she mumbled.

"What? What is it? What the fuck?"

"I said I always wanted what you had, Vann. Don't you get it?"

"Are you gay? Are you coming out to me right now?"

"No. I don't know. I just felt cheated, like if I could have been happy without having to get pregnant..." Her voice waivered and she swiped away an errant tear.

"This is insane, Lisa"

"It makes perfect sense, actually."

"In what crazy town is that?"

"I wanted to be happy like you were happy. I wanted that for myself." She looked at me pleading, eyes full of tears.

"Everyone wants to be happy, Lisa." I dug some fast-food napkins out of the glove box. "Just being gay or falling in love with a woman doesn't guarantee that. It's a job, you have to work at it. Where is all this coming from?"

"When you came home today talking about her brother, I was mad at you."

"Mad at me?"

"For ruining my fantasy life."

"How did I ruin your life? Maru left me remember."

"I know that, but I thought that if you were happy, I could be one day too."

"You can; you will, Lisa."

"It just seems impossibly far away. I have two girls and I am not going to turn into our mother. I can't do that to Mike anyway. There's just no way for me to ever have what you have."

"Don't say that. Look at Dad. He turned it all around, didn't he?"

"Dad? Yeah, he sure did."

"Well, why can't you; why can't I?

"You already have, twice."

"Lisa, I have no idea what I'm doing. I thought I had it together and was just blissfully plodding along with this easy, perfect life when I got the holy shit kicked out of me. There are no guarantees. You just keep grinding it out hoping for the best."

"Is that what you call it? Grinding it out. It looks a lot more like flitting about all happy and free."

"Flitting about? Now that's funny" I goaded a smile. "This is uncharted waters for me, Lisa. I don't have any answers here. I've never been so scared of losing it all while being so close to authentic happiness. It's terrifying."

"You've always been so together. You're saying you're a fake."

"Oh no, I believed I had everything under control. Even when I moved out of the house, I had my sights on UCLA. I was determined and fearless. When I graduated, I was already going on to grad school. And before I got my masters, I met Maru and we were starting this—this life together. I thought I knew what was going on; thought I knew everything.

Then she disappears and I was absolutely trashed. I couldn't breathe or think or move. I was completely lost. I was pathetic. And just when I thought I was picking up the pieces and truly revealing myself, Daisuke happened. And I can't even say he happened, because I made him happen to me. Even though I'm aware that he was a façade for the one I really wanted, I fell for him anyway. I mean, how fucked up is that?

Now this whole thing with Dad. I have no idea what I'm doing and honestly, if we're being totally honest here, for the first time in my life, I'm aimless and afraid."

"Really? "

"Can I make this shit up? No way."

"That is really messed up, Vann."

"I know right?" We tried to laugh. "But I still believe I can be happy, happy again, some way, some day. I can't ever go back to Princess Oblivion, but I'm not sad about that. She was a bitch anyway."

"Are you calling yourself a bitch? I can confirm that."

"Thank you for agreeing with me, I think." We were both rolled a chuckle into a belly laugh. We calmed down and stayed quiet for a moment.

"You were my hero, not Dad." Lisa's voice shook. "It was when you left that I felt abandoned—totally exposed."

"Oh, Lisa, I'm so sorry I hurt you that way. I never meant to, never thought it was that bad back home. You were always so damned resilient."

"What choice did I have?"

"You're right. I could have been there; I could have been a better big sister."

"Why don't you try being my sister now?"

"Now? Now that I'm a total train wreck and you're the one giving advice?"

"Yeah. You're at your best when you're vulnerable. Be my big sister now."

"Vulnerable? I guess I am defenseless after all this."

"Yes, and more tolerable, too."

"You can stop kicking me while I'm down anytime."

"Ok, I'll let you know when I'm done."

"Haha. How am I supposed to be a sister to you now?"

"Jeez, Vann. You're still Princess Oblivion."

"I honestly don't know what you're fishing for here."

"I'm not fishing, I just want my best friend back." Her words sank deep into my maternal instinct. I ran my hand through her hair and tucked a curl behind her ear.

"Of course. I'm here now." My voice was low and melodic to soothe her. When she looked over at me, her eyes big and wet, I saw the same heart-wrenching face she had when I left for college. I tried to smile, but my lips were quivering out of control. "God, I love you."

"I love you too."

"I'm glad we're doing this together."

"Me too." We were quite for a long time while tears dried up and miles skipped along under the truck.

"You don't really want to leave Mike, do you?" I asked.

"I don't know. My whole life is so bland, oatmeal every day. I want color and excitement, you know."

"Whether you stay with Mike or leave him, it all turns to oatmeal, Lis. A new relationship, a new job, a new baby, whatever. You either find happiness where you are, or you don't."

"I guess I'm the latter then."

"As am I at the present. But I'm learning; I'm figuring some things out."

"Like what?"

"Like love is a slippery, vicious thing."

"So, you don't want to be in love?"

"Of course I do. I just can't pretend it's all simple and lovely. It's a freak show: sometimes exciting, sometimes terrifying but always entertaining."

"I guess I've never experienced anything exciting or entertaining about love."

"You still can."

"How's that? I'm married with 2.5 kids and a dog."

"Have you tried opening up to Mike? Let him know what you like or want to try?"

"Not really. I've always been afraid he'd leave me if I complained or asked too much of him."

"Well, having recently been left, I can attest that it's survivable. And could possibly be positive. Just saying, it definitely feels like the end of the world. But it's not. There's life on the other side of divorce. Plus, it may never come close to that. Who knows? Maybe Mike has been waiting for you to unload all this time. Maybe he'll suggest a threesome or something."

"Gross, Vann."

"I take it you've never tried one. You wouldn't call it gross if you have."

"Totally gross."

"Well, what are you wanting, then Miss Priss."

"I'm not a priss; I just like romance and excitement."

"Romance and excitement, huh? How open-minded are you, exactly?"

"Pretty-open minded right now. I can't believe I'm telling you this, but I fantasized about not going home. Just saying 'fuck it' and starting over."

"Not cool. Very not cool."

"Oh, yeah, sorry. Too soon?"

"You don't want to do that to him or the girls. I won't let you anyway. I'm your big sister and I know that's not what you need to fix things."

"Ok then, what do I need?"

"You need to get drunk."

"That can't be the answer, Vann. Drinking causes more problems most of the time."

"Just tonight. We're going to go into San Fran and tie one on." I started searching on my phone for a place to dance. "We'll find someplace cool downtown, go out and have so much fun, you'll be ready to go home before you ever get there."

"I don't know, Vann."

"That's right! Don't know. Stop knowing right now. We're so doing this."

"What?"

"We're going down to Castro and have ourselves a good little time. I haven't partied in ages."

"Why start now?"

"Because you need to and as your best friend, I'm going to make sure you have a good time."

"What about Dad's funeral."

"It'll still be there when we get in tomorrow. Castro is only like 25 miles from Walnut Creek anyway. We'll still stay at the hotel Mike reserved and be back on the road in the morning to Tassajara."

"We can't just make up some crazy stuff to do, Vann. We barely—"

"The hell we can't. You said excitement. Here it comes." Her eyes looked leery, but she smiled broadly. "Just one night. Then you can go back to whatever you do that's whatever you do." She looked down the road still smiling and bumped the cruise control by 2 miles per hour. Whatever we were going, we'd be there four minutes faster.

Chapter 15

We bum-rushed a Jack in the Box in Redding and I took over behind the wheel. I set the cruise control at 9 over the limit, certain there was a fuel leak in the truck because we had stopped every two hours to pump another $80 into that thing. Lisa threaded together a 90's mix of our favorite songs from her phone and we sang at the top of our lungs all the way to Walnut Ridge.

We checked in just after 9 and spruced up in our room. Lisa fluffed her hair out of her ponytail holder when she saw me shimmy into the little black dress I wouldn't be needing for a funeral.

"Wait, are we supposed to dress up?" she asked.

"More like dress down, but you can wear whatever you want."

"Where are we going?"

"Lexington Club."

"A club? I didn't bring club clothes."

"Here," I threw her a pair of my favorite capris.

"You're too tall, I can't wear these."

"They'll be like high-waters. Trust me." I fidgeted with a button-down shirt, rolling up the sleeves and unbuttoning down to her sternum.

"I look like a weirdo."

"You look approachable."

"No guy is going to pick me up looking like this."

"We're not going to that kind of bar."

"Oh," she said with a hint of curiosity. "It's a gay bar."

"It's a girls' bar."

"What's the difference? You don't all go to the same bar?"

"Hell no, that's gross. Guys want to see other guys dicks or stick theirs in a rando hole in the wall. Girls want to dance and romance. You can't do that in the same place."

"I guess it never occurred to me."

"Me either until I found myself at a boys bar watching a bunch of cocks on TV's all over the place."

"Oh, that is gross."

"We're just going dancing and to have a good time. And you look hot."

"Really. I don't look mom-ish?"

"Not with the lights down low. Now come on." I saw a greedy smile on her face, but I wasn't sure. I just knew she was ready to have a good time, finally, and I was going to show her one.

We paid a small fortune for a cab over to the Castro district. I was glad they didn't charge a cover to get into the Lexington which was already packed by the time we got there near 11:00. The women were pressed closely, the whole room swaying to the beat the DJ spun from the corner. My heart rate picked up seeing all the Asian dykes grinding on the dance floor. I looked back at Lisa who looked so scared, like she might not go in.

"Let's go get a drink." I pulled her hand, but she resisted. "I'm right here," I reassured her. "You're going have fun as soon as you drop the baggage. Hold my hand and everyone will just think we're together." She relented and followed me inside.

I ordered myself the gold star and a pink panties for her. We slammed them at the bar and chased them with shots of Patron. I could see the buzz washing over her as she started to relax. The DJ was killing it and I couldn't stay still any longer. I kissed her cheek and pulled her into the throng of pulsing women.

She looked around wild-eyed and eked out a meager dance-like motion.

"Just watch me," I mouthed at her. Yelling over the music would have been a waste. "You're fine." I may have showed off for any wondering eye, but my end game was to loosen her up. A blonde dressed in little more than tassels and briefs came by with a tray of Jell-O shots. I threw a $5 on the tray and took two. I mashed one in my mouth and handed the other to Lisa who watched in horror. She tried to gingerly lick the thing out of the cup and quickly relented. We were both twirled and laughed hysterically.

A dark-haired fem cruised up to us with a couple of drinks and offered one to Lisa. She yelled something in Lisa's ear who looked over at me for help. I signaled for her to tip up the drink. She sipped at it but started to dance with the fem anyway. I reassured her with a nod as a blonde dyke started grinding on me from behind. I pressed into her and worked it like a pole. The crowd closed between us. I hoped Lisa wouldn't come streaming from the pack in a panic as I pulled the pixie's arms around me.

On the way back to the bar, I saw my straight, sweet little sister pressed against the wall with her hand up another girl's shirt. I nearly walked over and snatched her up until I saw her face. I recognized her expression of release and halted. I told myself she was a grown woman, that I was the one who brought her here and it looked as if she was having a decent time. I wondered if she was feeling the same bewilderment and base desire I had felt when I mauled Daisuke the first time. By the look on what I could see of her face, she wasn't feeling anything except a hard nipple between her fingers and a soft tongue down her throat.

I ordered a double amaretto sour, took a long pull and waited for the toll to rush through me. Another trip to the dance floor and back to the bar and I was feeling quite fine myself. The beat was throbbing, the women were hot, and I was gliding. This wasn't dulling discomfort, but more like being fully in the moment. It was the first time in a very long time that I was just dancing, just seeing beautiful women, just feeling tipsy and not being drug down by Maru or over stimulated by Daisuke or depressed by my pathetic family life. It was easy. Nothing had been easy since 9:30 AM, 13 Saturdays ago.

Midnight rushed up like a cool breeze as I leaned my elbows against the bar. Lisa was a natural chick magnet, dancing in a circle of two or three women. It was tough to tell working through my fifth cocktail at the dance of delighted ladies. She was fresh blood in the water. Straight women were easy for seasoned Lesbians to tempt, especially after a couple of drinks. All this was good information I picked up after I had long fallen in love with Maru. What's the lure of a first timer? I'll never know, I thought, finishing off number five. I was just glad that I could see she was having a good time for the first time since we were little girls.

"Whatcha drinkin'?" A woman down the bar with a sweet southern drawl said just loud enough for me to hear over P!nk's latest hit. She faced the bartender holding a half-empty martini glass.

"Excuse me?" I said, wondering if she was talking to me since she wasn't facing my way.

"Can I buy you a drink, darlin'?" She was still looking at the back of the bar, long locks of golden hair hid her face from view. She was late 30's, early 40's and wearing a white one-shoulder shirt, dark skinny jeans with boots.

"Sure," I said moving down to a stool beside her. "I'll have what you're having."

"Bradford, straight," she told to the bartender.

"Hey thanks," I said. "I'm Vann."

"Alex," she said swirling her glass. "Is that Van, like a family car?"

"Oh no," I laughed a little. "It's a family name, though."

"Ahhh." She took another drink.

"Is Alex short for Alexandra?"

"I guess you could say it's a family name too." The words flowed out of her mouth like a lazy river, totally hypnotizing. "I must admit your repeated trips to the bar and dance floor have me intrigued."

"Oh, I came with a...friend, but it looks like she's found someone. I'm just having a good time."

"Are you now?"

"Yes ma'am, I am." My eyelids drooped with satisfaction when the bartender put the martini in front of me.

"Thanks Bert," she said to the bartender who moved down the bar.

"Her name is Bert?"

"Roberta."

"Ahhh, I see. Thanks for the drink."

"You're not from 'round here?" she asked still facing the wall of liquor behind the bar.

"No, L.A. Well, Vancouver just outside of Portland, but I live in L.A. now."

"Well, what are you doing up here?"

"Long story."

"Aren't they all?"

"Yes, indeed. You're not from here, I can tell by your accent."

"It tends to give me away. I am definitely a long way from home."

"Where's home?"

"It's here now." Cryptic, I thought. "Is that a dress you're wearing?"

"Yes…" I leaned back from the bar, thinking she hadn't had a good look before.

"Doesn't sound like the usual denim around here."

"Excuse me?" She tossed her hair over shoulder revealing a tan face and pair of white-framed glasses. But they weren't like anything I'd seen before. The lenses were clear, but reflective at the same time.

"Look around. You won't see a lot of skirts or dresses out there? It's classy. I like it." I wheeled around trying to force myself from staring.

"Don't guess so."

"So, your 'friend'? I hope that's not a girlfriend who left you for finer pastures."

"No, she's my sister." I laughed at the misunderstanding.

"She brought you to a girls' bar and ran off and left you?"

"Not exactly. I brought her." A smile crept over her face as she was putting it together. Her teeth were flawless and white. Actually, just about everything about her was perfection: her French manicure, passion-pink lips and sculpted shoulders. I looked lazily into her glasses, but she didn't look away this time. I Wear My Sunglasses at Night was playing in my head under the club music.

"Her first time?"

"Yup." I took another drink and looked for Lisa in the crowd. "She's the one with the small army of drooling Lesbians around her." Alex nodded but didn't surf the crowd.

"I'm sure."

"So…" I said as nervously as drunk would let me be. "What's with the shades? It's pretty dark in here." She was still smiling when she turned fully to me and pulled them off.

"Window dressing." Two impossibly clear blue eyes looked past me. They were a little deep set, but nothing you would notice unless you were close.

"Oh, I'm sorry. I didn't realize you were—blind."

"Legally, yes. I see some shapes and figures. And don't be sorry." She slid the glasses back on.

"Wow, that's...wait. How did you know it was me coming back to the bar?"

"There's a lot more about you, Vann, than how you look."

"My god, that's amazing."

"The first think I noticed was your perfume. Then your dress. I was curious, I guess."

"You can hear my dress? That's really incredible."

"Your dress, your voice when you ordered a double amaretto sour. Honestly, I thought you must be a straight girl, but..."

"Well, that's currently complicated."

"Currently complicated? Now I'm even more curious."

"Me too, Alex." I looked down at her hand on her knee. I don't know what I was thinking, maybe about Maru's heart beating through her chest. Don't see, just know. I reached for it tentatively. "There's a pattern in this dress. Do you want to..." I trailed off closing my hand over hers. I guided her to the hem which was well above my knee when seated. I absolutely reveled in watching her face delight as her fingers explored the intricate stitching. I imagined myself seeing this dress for the first time one square inch at a time.

"Is it...leaves? The outlines of leaves?"

"Yes! That's so cool." I felt a tingling chill shiver through my body as she surveyed the spaghetti straps and low-cut neckline.

"Oh, that is hot." She said and brought her hand back to her empty martini glass. "Thank you."

I saw Lisa feeling her way along barstools and the people on them toward me.

"Hey!" I said, reaching my arm around her waist.

"This is fucking great, Vann! I haven't had this much fun—"

"Ever?" She nodded. "I'm glad. You deserve it. This is Alex. Alex, this is my little sister, Lisa." She gave a wave at Alex and made a face at me.

"Don't call me your little sister. It makes me feel like a kid."

"Well, kid, you are younger and shorter."

"My God, you two are sisters!" Alex laughed

"Oh, fuck you," Lisa said. "I'm going to go back to the hotel." She grinned broadly.

"Are you ready to go already?"

"Oh yeah." I explicitly remember her licking her lips right then.

"But not with you."

"I don't know, Lisa. Are you sure that's a good idea?" I was sobered by concern for something stupid my sister might do and regret later.

"Yep." She leaned in nearly laying over my shoulder. "I got a ride with Jenna." She thumbed over her shoulder at a red-headed pixie, wearing leather pants.

"Is she sober? Is she even old enough to drive, Lisa?" I eyed the girl up and down seeing her eyes locked on Lisa, keys already in her hand. "You're pretty drunk. Do you want me to come with you?"

"I don't need a chaperone. She's sweet. And we're just going to get some coffee and talk."

"Yeah, right."

"Whatever, Vann. You don't get to tell me what to do," she pouted.

"You're right. I just don't want you to do something you're going to regret."

"I've regretted my whole life, V." She looked at me with fiery intensity.

"Let her go, Vann." Alex said. "She's ready to go." I shot her a look and instantly felt like an idiot since it made no difference.

"Thank you, Alex. I am ready to go."

"You go straight to the hotel and text me when you get there," I said squeezing her hand to get the remaining morsels of her attention. "Promise me."

"I promise."

"Before any article of clothing hits the floor, Lis. Promise me."

"I promise," she whined.

"Sweet Jesus, Vann. She's a grown woman," Alex shook her head. Lisa nodded at her, oblivious. "With two girls and a husband back home," I thought. But she was right; I didn't get to tell her what to do. I was a recent expert at failure in that department.

"Be smart; be safe." I said pulling her in for a hug. She kissed my cheek and nearly ran to the outstretched arm of her impending lay.

Turning back to Alex, my mind ran wild. I tossed the last of my drink down the hatch.

"Ready for another drink?"

"I'm sure you are."

"I'll get this one. You up for a shot?"

"Make it a double and I'm in."

"Bert! Two red-headed sluts, double!" The sweetness lit a fire down my throat and overloaded my bloodstream almost immediately. We slammed the glasses down laughing.

"Do you dance?" I asked her.

"Me? I love dancing. It's just...uh...close."

"Tell me what to do. I want to dance with you." Bert looked over at me scowling. I tried getting some kind of permission from her, but it was nothing but skepticism on her face.

"Everything ok, Alex?" She said, wiping her way down the counter to us.

"Hold my bag, Bert?" She slung a large purse up from her barstool.

"You sure, Alex?"

"Just fine. Vann and I are going to do a little dancing." I smiled spitefully at Bert, the butch bartender, bouncer, bodyguard, and bitch.

"Yeah, we're going to tear up the dance floor." My inhibitions were audible.

"Take me to a place by the wall." She pointed to the far side of the bar. I laced my fingers through hers and pulled her off the stool. Gliding behind me, she wrapped her other hand around my hip. We weaved like a Chinese dragon through the crowd to where she had indicated.

"Ok, what do I do?"

"Dance, baby! Just don't let go." She kept one or two hands on me and moved in effortless rhythm against my body. She tossed her hair across my face, sending the smell of hibiscus through my numbed senses. I tried closing my eyes and just feeling her movements, but the buzz was too strong and made me stumble badly. She righted me, laughing.

"You are some kind of strong," I yelled over the music.

"You are some kind of drunk!"

"That I am." I laughed too. The DJ mixed one track into the next. We could have been the only girls on the floor. It was intimate, not like random chicks getting off on the gyrations of a stranger. I was fairly certain she already knew everything about me somehow and I was remembering everything about her as the night unfolded.

I shoved both my hands in her back pockets and pulled her into my chest. The pulsing strobe made her shifting shapes look electric. She turned toward the stage, and I saw it. I froze, my heart seized in my chest. Even upside down I knew exactly what it was: an opened white lotus on her left shoulder blade. The tattoo of the woman in my dream from 13 Saturdays ago.

She bumped into me awkwardly still moving with the music.

"You ok?" She yelled in my ear. My eyes went out of focus as every inebriated cell in my brain locked on the delicate outline.

"Uh, yeah. Just déjà vu."

"Oh, I hate it when that happens. You want a Jell-O shot?" I looked over my shoulder and saw the fem with the tray making her way back toward our corner.

"How did you?"

"Cherry Jell-O, maybe strawberry?" I inhaled deeply and could pick up the faint scent of sweetness over the bodies and booze.

"You are fucking wicked," I said twisting myself around in her arms. I threw my head back over her shoulder and pushed her hands down to my waist. The bass pounding under the beat swung us together in rhythm. She felt like skinny-dipping. I felt like no one and everyone at the same time. Just melting into this woman and the dance floor and the sound waves.

When I thought my legs would not hold me up anymore, the house lights flickered, collecting my attention.

"What's that?"

"What? Oh, what time is it?" I pulled her arm up to look at her watch. It didn't have any numbers on it.

"I can't tell. Your watch..." She flipped the face up and touched the dials. I pulled my phone from my pocket. The light from the screen nearly blinded me. One unread message from Lisa.

"Almost two. Last call. You want anything from the bar? We better get it now."

"Oh good! Lisa made it back to the hotel."

"I guess you need a place to crash then."

"Guess so."

"Let's get out of here." She snapped in behind me almost pushing me over. We collected her bag from Bert who gave me the stink eye when I pushed the door open and tumbled out into the night laughing. The fresh, wide-open air blasted our faces.

"I'll hail us a cab, unless you're sober enough to drive," I said laughing at my own joke. She pulled a collapsible cane from her bag and snapped it straight.

"No need. I always have a ride." Headlights lit up the reflective tape on her cane and a cab pulled out in front of us.

"Oh, how do I get one of those?" I dripped with jealousy.

"You don't want to know."

"Oh sorry."

"I said, don't be sorry." She said smiling and pulling me into the cab.

"Same place as usual, Miss Howe?" the driver asked.

"Yes please."

"Miss Howe? Alex Howe." The driver looked at me in the rearview mirror.

"Yeah, so?"

"So what?"

"Just the one passenger tonight?" the driver asked.

"Just one passenger? How many do you usually bring home?" I asked bewildered.

"Yes, Marco! Thank you. I said you don't want to know." Her southern accent pulled in an extra syllable to kno-ow.

"You said don't be sorry. Am I going to be sorry?"

"Are you?" She pulled me across her and kissed me laughing. Her hand had no trouble finding its way up my dress. I inhaled sharply and snapped upright.

"Alex!" I squealed and lowered my voice. "The cab driver."

"So?"

"So just because you can't see him, doesn't mean he can't see you...and me." I whispered too loud with urgency.

"Marco? He doesn't care?"

"I'm sure he doesn't."

"You do?"

"A little," I strained.

"Oh sorry. We can just sit here like good little girls," she said smacking of sarcasm. She sat up off me straightening her blouse and smoothing out my dress. Carlos smiled into the windshield. "I mean, I'm sure if he sees you in public he's going to point and laugh."

"Fuck you," I said giggling.

"Oh, I plan to." She whispered in my ear.

"Did you catch that, Carlos?" I threw my voice to the front seat.

"No ma'am," he said. But I could tell by his grinning.

"You are so bad, you bad girl." I breathed into her neck.

"Whaaaat?" she feigned. "I'm a southern lady."

"Sure, you are. All southern comfort, I bet." Her hand was back on my thigh, creeping upward.

"Carlos is very discreet; my best driver." She pulled my hand up her shirt. I could feel her laughing silently through her chest.

"Wicked indeed..."

Back at her apartment, another bottle of wine later, I was shifting through the movements of her hands and body heat. She was so familiar, like my favorite Italian dish, mushroom risotto, smooth and decadent. I was unthinking and uninhibited, like meeting an old lover after a long time apart. I don't remember everything, but mostly how she felt me with every part of her body as we twisted together. I remember piercing through alcoholic fog her two orgasms, loud and delicious against my chest, and then feeling a deep luxury satisfaction of love well made.

Chapter 16

It was maybe two hours later when I woke up alone, the white sheets billowing from the open window. Up on my elbows, I saw her drift quickly across the bedroom, the lotus tattoo slipping between the hanging sheets.

"Alex?"

"Be right back!" she called. It was a studio apartment. One of the sheets angled across the open floor from her bed to the bathroom. The other cut across to the kitchen and strong smell of coffee where she had oozed off to. It all came crashing together. It was like a nod from the cosmos, deep in my chest. That dream, that fucking haunting dream from 9:30 13 Saturdays ago spiraled into focus. I didn't understand it and knew I wouldn't ever have an answer. But it all made sense somehow.

She was back with two mugs of dark coffee. "Hope you like it black."

"Like tar," I said. It was fresh ground, stabbing as it went down. "Perfect." She crawled back in bed completely naked beside me. By daylight she was breathtaking. All-woman, all-fem and completely unbridled.

"You have no idea how beautiful you are, do you?"

"Neither do you, Vann Townsend." She said deliciously kissing my neck.

"Touché." I put down my coffee and stretched long like a cat. "It is so freaking early."

"Almost 6 a.m. When were you and Lisa planning on getting back on the road?"

"How much did I tell you last night?" I didn't remember much conversation going on.

"Your dad's funeral at the Buddhist place in Tassajara?" She tried jogging my memory.

"I told you about that?"

"You don't remember? How funny."

"Funny for you, maybe. Maybe I don't want you to know all my secrets."

"Oh, baby. It's too late. You gave them all up last night."

"Haha. No seriously, how were you not drunk? That's so unfair."

"I have to mind my buzz, I guess. Professional hazard."

"Did you tell me what you do for a living that allows you to stay out until 2 a.m. on a Thursday and sleep with whomever you like, sometimes in multiples?"

"Don't think we got around to that."

"Well?" I took another drink of coffee and her flawless figure.

"I own a software company. We design accessibility apps."

"No kidding? What a coincidence."

"What, because I'm blind. How is that a coincidence?"

"No, I'm a programmer for Houlihan Lockey."

"Well, that is a convenient coincidence."

"I thought I was like the only Lesbo programmer nerd on the face of the planet."

"Who you callin' nerd? Nerd?"

"No. I'm just saying..."

"Don't try backing out of that one."

"Ok. You're right. But you have got to be the hottest, sexiest, business nerd I have ever pressed my ever-lovin' inches against," I said in my best exaggerated country accent.

"And how many of those—"

"Ok, just the one." We laughed into our mugs. "Ugh! I don't want to go!" I pulled the sheets up around me.

"Are you coming back through this way?"

"Yes, but we're not stopping on the trip home. Do you ever get down to L.A.?"

"I think you knew this was one of those things, Vann."

"One of what things?"

"One of those one-time things? I thought that's what you were looking for at the bar."

"I wasn't looking for anything at the bar. I'm not a one-time kind of gal, really."

"Are you kidding me?"

"Seriously. Is that—oh, I feel really stupid."

"No, no. Please don't think that. I just don't have a lot of...return visitors." I felt immediately awkward. Like Eve realizing she was naked, I started pulling on the remnants of my outfit. "Vann? I can tell you're getting dressed. Please don't think..."

"Think what? I don't know what to think. I mean honestly. What was I thinking?"

"We had a good time; you're a great dancer; and amazing in bed."

"I don't need a pep talk, Alex. It's fine. I just thought I knew you. I really thought I knew you somehow, but now I feel really stupid." She worked her way around the bed toward me where I was about to give up looking for my panties.

"Don't feel stupid. Don't say that. It's me. It's me." She found me and pulled me up from the floor.

"How is it you?"

"Really, I think you can figure it out."

"Because I wasn't feeling stupid enough? I don't get you. Why did you buy me a drink? Why did you bring me here and...and?"

"It was a drink, Vann. No one has ever bought you a drink? Besides, you didn't have a lot of options with your sister and the girl she took off with."

"So. You didn't have to fuck me. I mean, you were all over me."

"It's just the thing."

"What thing!" I was exasperated, feeling angry, hurt and confused but at the same time petty and foolish.

"I'm a novelty lay, Vann," she popped off. I went rigid in her arms. "Come on. Don't tell me you didn't want to sleep with me just to see what it would be like."

"No, that's awful. What the fuck is a novelty lay?"

"Well, no wonder you're so pissed."

"So, what, you just pick up women and turn them loose after one night?"

"It didn't start that way. I got hurt a couple too many times and just built this emotional wall as a self-preservation mechanism. I gave up on an actual relationship years ago."

"Now I feel like an ass."

"No. Don't say that. It's sweet, really. Just not a lot of people see this as a long-term situation. I've gotten used to it, I guess. I'm sorry I hurt you."

"I just saw this amazing, amazingly hot woman who can dance and make me feel like the whole world. Who wouldn't want that in a 'long-term situation?'"

"Just kiss me now."

"What?" I turned my face to her, appalled. She landed her mouth on mine anyway. I resisted at first and gave in, knowing it was the last.

"Vann, I would love it if you never left. But I know you have a life out there and you have to go, for now."

"I really do have to go. This feels so...unfinished."

"Maybe it is. If you make it back this way, find me. And your panties are between the sheets at the foot of the bed." It was unfair; I felt like the one with the disability. How is it possible to tell someone is not wearing panties by kissing them? I thought about telling her to keep them, but they were my favorite pair, so I fished them out and slipped them under the dress.

"So, what, does Carlos discreetly pick me up now?"

"I already called Stevie to take you to your hotel. Carlos is my night driver."

"Wow, do you own a taxicab company too?"

"They're on retainer. I really can't drive."

"How convenient." I wanted to uncover her. I wanted her to feel as naked and vulnerable as I did. "I really thought you were into all that last night." I said sitting on the bed. She sat up next to me.

"You felt it too?"

"Yes, I did! I felt everything and now it feels like you're telling me it was fake."

"It wasn't. You know it wasn't. Don't be upset, Vann."

"How can I not be upset?"

"Just remember this."

"That's just it, Alex. I remembered this before it ever happened. And you felt so comfortable like I had known you all my life. So, I'm feeling all betrayed and over-reacting and I don't even know why."

"Maybe it's your subconscious telling you this was supposed to happen."

"That's what it felt like when we were dancing last night. That's what it felt like when you were screaming in my ear, twice."

"I know, I felt it too."

"Then what's with the brush off?"

"I get to be scared too." I tucked a blonde lock behind her ear and tried to register in her gaze. She reached for my hand and kissed my fingers. "Don't you think if this was supposed to happen, then it will happen again?"

"Ok, you can just kiss me now," I relented, only don't know-ing. And she kissed me over and over with such ferocity, I knew her all over again.

Stevie was too soon, and I pulled away from her reluctantly like hands in prayer position.

"You have to call me," she said slipping a card into my purse at the door. "Call me, please." I felt the raised dots Brailed on the back of the card.

"If I'm supposed to." She smiled and settled back on her heels.

"Talk to you soon then, Vann Townsend."

Chapter 17

I jammed my hotel card in the slot and pushed open the door flooding the darkened room with the light of 1,000 suns. The pixie girl shot up from the queen bed across the room. Lisa groaned and pulled the comforter over her head.

"Jesus, Vann! Turn off the light."

"The light is not on Lisa, and you need to get up. Sorry, Jenna, we have to go."

"No-o." Lisa whined.

"Ye-es," I mocked her pouting. "You two have until I get out of the shower and it's bye-bye time. Don't make me be the bad guy."

"Too late," she mumbled pulling the girl who was attempting to flee the scene back under the covers. "Coffee."

"You coffee; I shower. We have to go to our father's funeral today, Lisa. Please, don't do this. I don't want to fight you."

"Who turned you into a bitch last night?" She scowled in my direction, blinded by hangover.

"I was already, remember?" I took my shower bag into the bathroom and made quick work of rinsing the deeds of the night. My toothbrush felt divine in my mouth, and I didn't want to imagine what my kisses tasted like. Metallic mustard? I could still smell Alex on my dress; my eyes lingered on the leaf pattern she had traced with her fingers. I didn't know if I was coming or going. I was freshly raw walking into a salt rubbing. Feeling worn, I opted for the cargo shorts I'd brought, a polo, cap and sandals for the rest of the drive.

The steam from the shower rolled out into the room when I emerged from the bathroom. I huffed. Lisa and Jenna were back asleep, sans coffee. Zero progress had been made.

"Dammit, Lisa!" I grabbed the comforter and pulled it off them both. "Do you have any idea what people do on these things? They're disgusting!" The girls squirmed like worms to cover themselves with each other leaving a creature with two butts protruding from four legs and arms.

"Your sister is fucked up," I heard Jenna say in a surprisingly deep voice for such a small body.

"That's right, Jenna. And this is you getting the fuck out of here back to whatever home wrecking you were doing before you found wasted little Lisa here."

"Back off, Vann!" Lisa sat up naked. "You are not in here. You don't know this."

"I have no clue what you're talking about. I really just want you to rinse some of that sex funk off you before we go get Dad. The shower is warm; go get in it!" Lisa marched passed me dragging the sour-faced pixie to the bathroom with her.

"I'm getting us coffee. Please be ready when I get back. Fifteen minutes, tops." I heard her mimicking me in the bathroom and giggle as I closed the hotel room door behind me. I felt responsible for this but clueless about what to do. We go get Dad, but then what? What next? I go home and tell Daisuke that I slept with a feral blind woman and led my sister into a hookup trap. She goes home and starts a threesome swingers club with Mike. Fairly certain I had just ruined at least 8 lives last night with a momentary lapse of my reliably safe (sic boring) judgment. Whatever seams that had been holding me together were threadbare. Wisdom: that mother-fucking thing you get right after you needed it most. I manhandled the espresso machine and produced a crème so fine, the rest of the shot was pure sludge. I found two cups of coffee for the girls and hammered another shot of espresso.

"You have to call me," she had said. And "please." Alex wouldn't have my number unless I called her. Until I called her. I reeled. I was not this person I had become. Since Maru, even including her, I was smashing into any and every person who showed any interest in me. This wasn't my style. I preferred calculated probability of success. Even Kate pointed out my formula for this very thing.

Every time I checked my phone I had no messages from Daisuke, and I sent none. What was this? Maybe he didn't want to do the hard stuff. Maybe he had to work a double. Maybe he knows if I got within ten feet of anything fuckable, I would buckle.

With Dad gone and everything I knew about him teetering perilously on manufactured narrative that leaned toward me being an insolent child of spite, the ground beneath my feet listed dangerously listing. With all the momentum of the past 13 Saturdays pushing me toward this final leg of my journey, I crashed like a pinball into everything, so obviously trying to slow the inertia of truly knowing myself for who I am.

I was already crying when I got back to the room with not enough hands to hold their coffees and open the door. "Open the door," I wailed. I could hear the shower still on and knew they would be pressed with passion in the gauzy clouds of steam.

I sat down next to the coffees and pulled my phone from my back pocket. No messages, no missed calls, no nothing. Just the outrageous time 7:07 reminding me how alone I was. The only real family I had was in the shower getting fucked by someone she would never see again. I suddenly saw how desperate and pathetic I had become. And being totally aware of my depraved position, I dialed up Daisuke. Too many rings, then voicemail. I pulled together my best I-haven't-been-crying voice and hold on to it before it burst out anyway.

"Dai, we're getting ready to leave San Francisco for Dad's funeral. It'll be today, I have no idea what to expect. I just wanted to let you know we're ok and that I wanted to talk to you because you make me feel better. You're probably working, but please call when you get a chance. I don't know when I'll be able to talk after we get to Tassajara. Just...just call me this morning when you get this. Bye." I ended the call and hung my head between my knees. I pulled the Brailed card from my purse and lightly ran my fingers over the raised dots.

Alex Howe—Consultant/Owner. I wanted to memorize Alex Howe in Braille, but the bumps were blurry through tears. I could smell her on her business card. I faked my best smile and let myself in the room.

"Coffee's in the hall ladies." I was met with curious looks, but they picked up the mugs in the hallway while I started packing everything that wasn't already on Lisa's body. I was determined to leave the place and the whole thing behind in rapid fashion, even as Lisa lingered.

How could I not empathize with her some in remembering my first time with a woman? If anyone had tried to run Maru or me out of that love den, they would have been shot. It was just bad timing. Tassajara was waiting for us to get there and could not wait another day. The finality and urgency seemed like an oxymoron. I couldn't help but think that was the first time I had been with a white girl, just like Daisuke had expressed with amazement. The loose ends weren't loose. They knotted together in my stomach, buckling my knees. The only way I knew to handle it was to get out of there.

The truck was loaded, and I sat in the driver's seat, transmission in drive. Lisa plodded across the hotel parking lot trying to put on a shoe and make it to the gurgling truck before I left her on the asphalt.

"We're leaving, now."

"Would you please let me get my shoes on?" She wrestled them on from the side of the truck and I could see Jenna barefoot in a white tank top and pair of boxers barreling into her. They collided with a smack and Lisa flattened across her husband's truck seat with frantic kisses from the pixie.

"Call me. As soon as you can. I'm so sorry about your Dad. You'll be ok." Jenna was rapid-firing reassurances between kisses.

"I'll call you as soon as I can, I swear. I swear." They were so cute, completely oblivious to the universe tilting around them.

"She'll call you, Jenna. Bye!" I pressed the gas pedal with the door still open and Jenna still trotting along beside it. Their cord was cut and I felt slingshot onto the freeway south to Tassajara.

Lisa slapped my shoulder hand-over-hand, crying and mumbling incoherently.

"Put on your seatbelt, Lisa." I fended her off with an elbow since I was a lousy stick-shift operator.

"What is wrong with you!" She screamed but clicked in the belt anyway. Being my passenger was no joke. A friend once told me 'you make the seatbelt tight,' when driving to a girls' kayaking trip.

"Are you serious? This whole situation is insane, Lisa."

"You did this, Vann. You did."

"I know I did this. Don't you think I feel horrible about it?"

"Why do you feel bad? I thought you wanted me to have a good time. And that's what I did."

"That's exactly what I wanted. I wanted you to get some drinks, let loose, dance a little without having the pressure of some mouth-breathing Neanderthal trying to pick you up or slip you a roofie. I didn't want you to wreck your marriage."

"Wreck my marriage? What does this have to do with my marriage?"

"You just fucked a woman...all night apparently and then again in the shower."

"My god, it was fantastic. I can't believe you held out on me all this time."

"Listen to yourself. This is not you. You're married and have two great little girls."

"You hate my girls, Vann. Don't even try to fake it."

"I don't like anybody's children. That's why I have a dog. That's not the point."

"So, we went out and had fun. I still go home. I still have to be a mom and a wife and a total waste. I still have to bury my father."

"What was all that shit about 'call me, call me'? You just cheated on Mike."

"I don't know. It's not the same."

"Don't tell me sleeping with a woman is not the same thing as cheating on your husband. It's insulting."

"Who do you think you are? Let's see, are you cheating on your wife with her brother? Or cheating on him with the bronzed blonde from the bar."

"That's so unfair."

"Welcome to the party, sister. I wasn't expecting any of this. I mean, Jenna was so—"

"I'm sure she was fucking amazing, and I don't want to hear about it."

"No really, she did this thing with her—"

"I said I don't want to hear about you fucking some little girl you picked up last night. Really, I don't. I just want to leave this place behind."

"What happened to you last night? You're different today. You were all 'you deserve to be happy, blah blah blah' yesterday."

"I don't know, Lisa. I keep saying that, but I really don't know what happened."

"Well, you didn't come back to the hotel."

"Did I have a choice?" I cut my eyes at her.

"I don't think I would have noticed." I could see her eyes glassing over reveling in whatever madness had ensued. And I'm sure it rocked her world just like it did mine. Had she been in a different situation, she may well have gone eight years or more in a relationship with whomever had opened her eyes in that way. "It's not fair. Mike is nothing like that."

"Lisa, I said—"

"I know, I know. Did you not go home with the hottie at the bar?"

"I don't want to talk about that either."

"Oh now I'm really curious. You stayed with someone last night. Was it not her, what was her name...I was so wasted."

"Alex. Her name is Alex Howe."

"As in, Alex, how do you like your martini?"

"Yes, but with an E." She was looking at me with this long, suspicious glance.

"You're awfully sensitive about this Alex Howe, aren't you?"

"Yes, I am. Can we let it go?"

"See that makes me want to push you more. I'm guessing she didn't read you poetry all night."

"No."

"You're blushing. You totally slept with her! Why don't you want to talk about this? I told you about mine."

"And I said I didn't want to hear about yours. And I don't want to talk about last night. Please, Lisa. Just let it go."

"Jee-sus, Vann. If we're not going to even savor the moment, what was it for?"

"You savor your moment. I'll just leave mine in San Francisco."

"It was that bad?"

"No, Lisa. It was freaking amazing and unexpected and I fucking fell for her in one night. Is that what you want to hear? And we slept, like two hours, and it was over. She showed me the door and gave me her business card and had her driver take me to the hotel. Her business card. Who does that?"

"Her driver? Who has a driver?"

"Stevie is on retainer. He was a very nice man."

"This is sounding weirder and weirder. Don't stop now. Stevie...her driver..."

"She's blind. Alex is blind." I looked away knowing what was coming.

"She what?"

"And she had amazing hands and mouth and...senses like you wouldn't believe."

"I'm sure. That explains the—well that explains a lot. And you fell for her? In one night? Is that even possible."

"No, it's not possible. None of that was possible. We danced for like two hours. It was like she knew every move before I made it."

"You were dancing?"

"Yes! That's what I'm saying. And then we went back to her place, and she was all over me and I was so drunk, I don't remember all of it."

"That's a shame."

"But I remember her and her—" I stopped short of opening that door.

"Her what?"

"Anyway."

"Her what?"

"Any. way. In the morning she made me coffee and told me to get out."

"What? Just like that?"

"What's a novelty lay?"

"Never heard of it."

"That's what she said. Like she has all these women for one night and she's ready for them to go in the morning. But I didn't want to go, and she seemed absolutely terrified by that."

"You're right. I shouldn't have made you talk about this."

"Well, too fucking bad, because we have four hours to figure it out before we have to bury our father. Or whatever it is that they're going to do."

"Cremation. It'll be a service and a cremation."

"Like a church."

"I don't know, Vann. I tried to look it up, but it looks like a funeral service."

"And then there's that. So yes, I am totally upside down and I haven't even got to the really fucked up part about it."

"You're kidding me, because it sounds like a train wreck already." I smiled and nodded.

"I dreamed about it. I shit you not, Lisa. I dreamed about her and her apartment and her lotus tattoo before it happened."

"No way. You're screwing with me, right?"

I shook my head. "That's why I'm so confused and not ready. I'm just not ready for what happened to me in there. Lisa, I dreamed about it the day Maru left me." She was speechless. Her mouth gaped. My eyes watered. "What does that mean? I am so psychotically confused."

"Oh my god, Vann. That is seriously, cosmically messed up."

"It was like making love to someone I've known my whole life. And she felt it too. I know she did."

"Like you had a past life together or something."

"I don't know what that is, but it's still burning in my stomach."

"Reincarnation. Maybe you knew each other before and were reincarnated to find each other just now, last night."

"I don't know which version sounds more psychotic. All I know is that I had to come get you and drive away and I don't really know what happened."

"It's terrible timing. But hey, if we weren't driving through to Tassajara, you wouldn't h have even been there last night." I wiped my eyes with my palm.

"I shouldn't have brought this up. I'm more confused, more frustrated and—"

"And more scared it sounds like. What about Daisuke? And then there's the whole topic of your missing wife. Now this?"

"I know. I haven't heard from him, and I don't know what that means. Maybe it's some family thing. If something happens, just disappear."

"Wouldn't that be messed up?" I laughed and she joined me.

"I just wish he would call me. He always makes stuff make sense."

"Would you tell him about Alex Howe?" she asked surprised.

"I think I would. I mean, it's not like we're in a relationship. We know what it is?"

"What what is? Like fuck buddies?"

"No. It's more intimate than that."

"But you're not in a 'relationship'?" She used air quotes.

"No."

"And you sleep together."

"Yes." I was irritated.

"More than once. Like, not a hookup."

"Yes. What's your point?"

"How is that not fuck buddies?"

"It's just not. And I am not giving you a sexual resume here."

"No, you're not being truthful to yourself. You just got out of a long-term relationship, if you're even out of it. And started sleeping with her brother."

"Ok. I get it. I feel so...so...traumatized. My entire system is in shock."

"Mine too. But damn."

"Am I in a relationship with Daisuke? Did I just cheat on him?" She nodded vigorously.

"You'll find out for sure if you tell him about Alex Howe."

"Stop calling her that."

"It's her name."

"Her name is Alex."

"Her name is Fucked You Up." I laughed out loud at that one.

"You're right on that one." We tried to soak it all in as the yellow lines blipped beside the truck.

"Are you going to tell Mike?" I asked after a while.

"I don't think so." She was wrung her hands playing out different scenarios.

"Will you call her?"

"I don't think I can."

"Why not?"

"I'd just want to see her again."

"It's just sex, Lis. It's not day-in-day-out, cotton panties, take out the trash. She rocked your world, fine. But can you really see her in your life, long-term."

"Just sex? You should take your own advice."

"That was different."

"Was it? You were together all of what, five, six hours? And it wasn't 'just sex'." Air quotes again. "Besides, you call it just sex when you've been married for four years to Mr. Three minutes on a good night."

"Oh jeez, that's bad."

"I feel so sorry for you and all the awesome 'just sex' you have. I had more orgasms last night than I've had the whole time with Mike."

"It was like that my first time, too."

"And you married her. That's insulting. 'Just sex'," she scoffed.

"But I wasn't already married with kids. But you made your point. I'm just saying I don't want you to throw away your life over a good lay. They make vibrators for that."

"Good lay? It was like the earth opened up and shot volcanoes out of my crotch. That's not a 'good lay.' And I have a vibrator." She was deadpan.

"Good for you."

"There's really no way for you to win this one."

"I can tell. Can we agree that we're both pretty screwed here?" She started laughing. Then I recognized the pun and started laughing too. It felt good. It felt real. "Just sex" can ruin lives and bring them together too. We both swam in uncertainty.

We played out different conversations we would never have, each playing opposite the other. When we'd had a healthy dose of reality, teetering between laughter and tears, we found a radio station and let it do the talking for a while. Lisa dozed, finally feeling the toll of a wicked night and emotionally exhausting experience ahead.

I thought I would be tired but felt the crackle of electricity in my nerves and searing heat in my veins. All the momentum was pressing me toward Tassajara, past that and right over the edge of reason.

Chapter 18

The road to Tassajara Mountain Zen Center was a spiritual practice in itself. A treacherous, winding dirt road scratched into the last 14 miles of the final leg from Caramel Valley to the Ventana Wilderness. Switchbacks doubled back on themselves in places and hung over steep drops in others. Lisa was glued to the window letting me know exactly how close I was to driving off the side of our miserable lives while I white-knuckled the gear shift. Just that stretch alone took an hour of our four-hour trip from Walnut Creek. We evoked the name of Jesus and threw in a couple of Buddhas, just in case.

We pulled into a neat row of cars and already dreaded the trip down the mountain, whenever that would be. We looked at each other for a while like the answers were there somewhere, but the other of us wouldn't give them up.

"No matter what; we're in this together," I said. She nodded with me. "Don't leave me and I won't leave you."

"I'm not scared."

"I am a little. I don't know what to expect."

"I think that's just the point. We're here for Dad."

"And for each other."

"And for each other." I squeezed the handle and stepped out onto the dirt. I immediately regretted the sandals because my feet were soaked from the death-defying drive we'd just survived, and mud was making pies in between my toes. I grabbed Lisa's hand as we crossed the road like when we were girls back home. Maybe instinct, maybe I still needed her to need me.

As we approached a main hall, a short-legged, short-haired woman in black and brown robes strode up to us with both hands outstretched.

"Girls, welcome," she said with such genuine warmth I wondered if she thought we were someone else she knew. She folded us into a hug in her arms as if we were her long-lost children.

"We're here for—" I started.

"Timothy, yes, yes. We're ready for you." I was still a bit buzzed from our entrance but was able to catch her name was Linda, the director of the center. She glided toward the Great Hall explaining this was the beginning of their guest season and some of Timothy's Dharma friends had come to join us. She paused at the entrance of the hall and stepped aside leaving a pair of fabric clogs at the end of a neat row of shoes. Lisa and I looked at each other and quickly dispatched our shoes into the line.

Through the entrance, a semi-circle of people sat on cushions and pads on the floor with an opening at the altar at the far side. A large stone Buddha figure was seated with candles, flowers, bowls of water, incense and fruit organized on a lower level of the altar beneath his feet.

The large, open room was very Japanese-looking with wood floors, wood ceiling, paper lamps, square windows and of course, all the Buddhist paraphernalia. Near the altar was a huge bell, as round as a whiskey barrel, but shorter, mounted on an enormous cushion that was on top of a wooden pedestal. I imagined myself crawling into the bell and disappearing with a great gong.

She motioned for us to take a couple of cushions on the floor nearest the door and directly across from the altar. I was hoping to change once we got there to something more appropriate, but I wouldn't get the chance. A woman in black and green robes with white waves of hair sat in front of the altar. Her eyes were down but not closed. She didn't look up when we made our noisy entrance. The others in the circle wore plain clothes like ours, also sitting quietly. A few gave us encouraging smiles. I tried to imitate their postures, but I was uncomfortable and obvious. I relented and sat cross-legged like a kindergartener.

I thought we were going to come in and see our father. I thought we were going to have a little ceremony, spread some ashes. I had no idea what this whole magic circle was. I looked at Lisa for confirmation of craziness, but she was looking down with her hands folded in her lap. It was pretty clear this was not her first meditation rodeo and I realized I was truly the only outsider in the group. My own sister, who had been closer to our father, who probably learned how to sit like a respectable meditator, blended into the circle. I alone stuck out like a lop-sided pinecone among beautiful mountains.

The white-haired woman folded over in a deep bow and everyone in the circle bowed with her, except me. The people adjusted on their cushions, some stretching out legs and backs while the leader went around the room making eye contact with each of us. When she came to me, I resisted the heavy temptation to look away. She continued around the room connecting with each person in the circle. She breathed deeply in and out a few times before a man in light blue robes rang the giant bell sending a soul-throbbing gong through the room that felt like it covered everything with warm oil.

"Let us welcome our visitors, Lisa and Vann Townsend," the woman finally said. Everyone in the circle folded over like the closing mouth of a clam and rose together. I instinctively bowed in return, something I had seen Maru do a hundred times, but it wasn't the right time.

"Let us welcome the clear light of our brother Timothy as he transitions through this mode of existence. And through him, let us be reminded of teachings of the Buddha on impermanence and universal suffering." She paused again. I wanted to raise my hand like in class and ask a question but knew better. I looked at Lisa again who was watching her intensely just like everyone else. She introduced herself as the Abiding Teacher and a close friend to my dad during his recent years at Tassajara.

"For the benefit of his beloved daughters, as well as any of you who have not experienced them, I will give a brief orientation on our funeral ceremony and discuss the final requests of our brother." It seemed odd that she referred to him as their 'brother,' that this was his family, not me. These last years, they had been closer to him than I ever was. I wondered how 'beloved' I was. Maybe Lisa, but not me. In my shorts and V-neck T-shirt, I felt naked.

The bald man beside the bell shuffled up to the altar. He bowed, stepped closer and lit incense and candles. He took a few steps back and everyone bowed along with him, except me. Lisa looked at me from her bow giving me a wide-eyed 'just-go-along-with-it' look. I shrugged and forced in a short bow so that I came up with everyone else. Apparently, I had missed the instruction book at the door.

"Emily Dickinson said, 'to live is so startling, it leaves little time for anything else." She began, all eyes fixed on her. "Timothy will always be a favorite example of mine of someone who is so startled to be alive, he fully emulated the freshness of the present moment." Soft chuckles and nods circled. It sounded so foreign that they were talking about the guy I knew as Dad. I had to force myself to meet him anew after his death.

"In his passing, as with all loss, we are reminded of our long attachments to our friends and our own lives. Timothy reminds us of the great poet, Ikkyu, who conceived Red Thread Zen after leaving the monastery and spending his pilgrimage in the streets of poverty and grief, in brothels with bums, thieves and all manner of laypeople. He wrote to truly be awakened, you had to get away from the pristine monastic life and find equanimity in the midst of true human existence. True grit, as it were. Ikkyu's master, Kido, said that human beings were linked from birth to death by the red thread of passion and its bloody umbilical cord. And in this, Timothy celebrates the end of his red thread with us now." I couldn't help but think about my own gory umbilical cord stretching from day to day, sticky and wet, pulsing with my own mess.

She went on to explain that their tradition believed my dad had existed in a state of clear light for three days after death. During that time, monks and sangha members took turns with the body chanting prayers, lighting candles and offering flowers and fruit to encourage a good passing and precious human rebirth. Now that the three days had passed, it was time to return the remains to the soil, honoring the interconnectedness of all sentient beings and in communion with the earth's resources. In a brief fire ceremony, we would start the cremation pyre tonight which would have to be tended through the night. At dawn, his ashes would be collected and carried along a nearby trail to the Suzuki Roshi Memorial to be scattered. The funeral was designed to comfort the deceased more than for those left behind. He had not requested a specific place for his ashes to be spread, but the guiding teachers at San Francisco Zen Center agreed that was a suitable place as a way to honor Timothy and his place among them.

My father's final requests had been recorded in a letter he had written during a writing meditation some months before. He asked to respectfully request and allow Lisa and me to participate in the ceremonies, as well as spend whatever time we wished with his body before cremation. She wanted us to understand that Dad knew he was depriving us of the finality of a traditional burial and a place to visit, however, that was his full intention because he would be with us always.

Tears were already tumbling down Lisa's reddened cheeks. I wanted to reach out to her, to comfort her, but sat still, paralyzed on my cushion.

The Abiding Teacher addressed us specifically saying our father had wished for us to attend this circle and ceremony and to receive a practice interview. However, these were merely his final offerings to us, and we were not to feel required or obligated in any way.

Then she addressed just me, her body and face fully engaged with mine. "For his eldest daughter, he offered his deepest gratitude. Being gifted by her birth and early years, he said, her strength and fortitude as a young woman were an eternal inspiration to him while imprisoned and later in his practice." There was no stopping the tears from me after that. I felt genuinely moved by her sincerity, knowing those were the truest feelings of a man I would have felt privileged to have known.

"For his youngest daughter, he offered sweet joy and affection. Being a father to her only briefly, and her unconditional love were the greatest gifts of his meager existence." We were both blubbering when the director moved toward us setting a box of tissues between our cushions. One woman covered her mouth and tears slipped over her knuckles.

"And to his beloved sangha, Timothy expressed blessings of profound equanimity." She smiled broadly. "And many fine sunsets." Many smiled through tears. "At this point, you all are welcome to share any memories of our brother as a way to honor him or comfort each other during transition." She bowed again and everyone followed. It was quiet a moment before a round man with round glasses held his hands in prayer pose and bowed, followed by everyone else.

"I just want to say Tim made the best meals." Nods and smiles around at this. "And it didn't matter how many were here; he ran the kitchen like an orchestra. And I'll miss his gazpacho." The round man bowed again, followed by everyone. I think that was where I finally caught on. Someone else bowed in and shared about him helping during the 2008 Basin Complex fire, which most people laughed about. Not in on the joke, I took the brief respite from silence as an opportunity to blow my nose which was flowing as freely as my tear ducts.

A graceful older woman bowed in and beamed at us. "I want to say what an honor it is to finally meet his two daughters." The circle collectively nodded and smiled in our direction. "Timothy talked often about the impressive accomplishments of you, Vann. And about his granddaughters, Lisa. You both truly were a joy to him and a joy to hear about." She bowed out and a deep gong bellowed from beside the altar. After the sound faded another much older woman bowed in and talked about visiting him at San Quentin. She talked a long time about teaching him how to meditate and answering his many questions. It was evident she knew him the longest and they listened intently. She was funny, lightening the mood with goofy antics of how Dad had accidentally gone to the meditation practice instead of NA and on to the unlikely story of how he turned to Buddhism. When she finished, most of us were laughing, eyes drying.

After she bowed out, Lisa bowed in. My eyes bulged in surprise. She seemed so uninhibited where I was so reserved which was usually reversed.

"I just want to thank you all for welcoming us and allowing us to be a part of your sangha. Dad truly loved you guys and felt very much that SFZC and eventually this place saved him from more suffering in his life. Please know that he was, and now we, are truly blessed by you all and your practice." I was blown away. She was so brave and connected to all of them in this way. I watched her in awe as another person bowed in and said something really nice about us and Dad. I felt my neck tingling and butterflies in my stomach. I was going to bow in, and before I had a chance to stop myself, I had done just that.

I rose up and saw everyone looking at me, like they could not wait to hear whatever I had to say. And neither could I. I had no idea what I was doing or what I was about to say. I took a breath and my mouth opened like words were about to come out, but I was still in complete shock.

"I didn't know my dad," I heard myself saying. I looked at Lisa to bail me out, but she beamed at me—no help at all. "He...sounds like a really nice man." Some nodded, some smiled. I felt like an idiot and knew I looked terrible. I don't cry pretty in any way. I butchered their circle and had no way of stopping myself. "I didn't even know he was Buddhist until yesterday. And this is very awkward, I'm sorry." I knew there was a look of horror on my face, but there was no way out of this until I bowed out. I was screaming at myself to bow out, bow out!

"I'm sorry, I'm not sure what I'm supposed to say, which is really unusual for me. I'm sorry," I said for the third time wiping my eyes and took in a deep breath. "It seems like I didn't know anything about the person he had become, and I really, really regret that. But I'm just so thankful for the ability to know him in this way through you all. Hearing your stories about him; it makes me think he and I could have been friends. And I would have really liked that." My face crumpled into tears, and I bowed wishing I could disappear into the floor. Lisa was smiling and crying and squeezing my hand. Others sniffled and passed around tissues. It was quiet for a long time until another bell tolled, this time, for me. I felt it in my chest and quivering heart jarring loose all the hurt, anger and resentment. I felt a nasty cloud lift out of me like the sun burning off fog, and a sudden release. Feeling physically lighter and sitting tall on my cushion, I felt the air and lightness of what I can only assume was my father, surround me.

Chapter 19

I watched in horror when Lisa threw herself across our father's body. The fresh fruit placed by his side thudded to the ground. She cried saying 'I'm sorry' over and over again. I tried pulling her away by a flailing arm, but she twisted free.

"That's not our dad, Lisa." I tried again and was met with a look of ferocity that told me to back off and/or go fuck myself. I didn't understand this kind of frantic, frayed grieving. His body was there, but the man was gone. All the backstory and bullshit reduced to what others might remember. The secrets he would never tell were gone with the wind like his ashes would be by daylight. The urgency and finality had arrived, fully present in my face.

I didn't recognize him after so much time had passed. I didn't recognize him, because I had changed too. I wondered if this was my San Quentin, my bottom from which I would rise to humble beauty. Or was I still on the way down. Seeing Lisa experience the shock of losing a parent was wrenching. I didn't feel the same. I had merely lost the possibility of knowing someone. Seeing her then at that last hour, I had to wonder was it worth it to love and experience such loss. My heart ached to comfort her, but there was no empathy for a potential parent. Was it better to truly feel nothing? I searched myself and was filled with regret.

Regret for missing my opportunity to know Timothy Townsend. Regret for not being able to comfort my sister. Regret for the tightening spiral my life was coiling down. Regret for not seeing myself for what I truly was, for being so closed. Regret for my extensive self-preservation system that had proven too much a burden in the end. Lisa's regrets were only for more time, which for me would have made no difference.

I left her there, alone with our father--her dad. It was probably the best thing I could do for her and certainly best for myself. That fact stood out to me as my usual refuge—whatever was best for number one. I was disgusted and heaving for air as I sprinted outside.

The coolness stung my lungs bare feet. Hands on my knees, I squeezed my eyes shut, forcing back more relentless tears. Tassajara was a huge mirror and the beast it reflected was nuclear-powered delusion. I was no more clever or cleaner or faultless than my dirty heels on a road barely scratched into the earth. No better than anything or nothing.

I pulled my hair back and let out a guttural cry letting out a long, profane "Fuck!" I stumbled backwards a few steps and ended up on my back in the dirt. The jolt of the ground brought my surroundings back to me and I felt embarrassed. I threw my forearm across my eyes, hoping no one would notice the wretched, screaming and cursing woman who had thrown herself on the ground.

This whole scenario seemed impossible. I was supposed to have been making final arrangements for my father. I was supposed to write a check to have him disposed of and go back home to my life in L.A. He was supposed to go in the ground the way I knew him as he lived. But this was all fucked up. While I was living my perfect façade of a life, my father was preparing to subtly shock the shit out of me. I had done so many things wrong, I didn't know if I could make anything right.

Instead of maintaining my blissful mirage of happiness and success, I was laying on top of a mountain in B.F.E. California having a personal come-to-Jesus meeting with myself. Whoever Vann Townsend had become, she was no friend to me. I would not have played with her during recess, nor I would not have given two shits about her when I arrived, completely blinded by selfishness, onto the UCLA campus 14 years ago.

I uncovered my eyes and looked up at the soupy blanket of stars. So, so many, so, so far away. And I remember suddenly feeling small—an impossibly minute speck on an insignificant rock barely protruding into a tiny corner of space.

Just then, the director bent over me and smiled.

"Would you care for some tea?" Tea? My mind was blank with embarrassment. She extended her hand from the long sleeve of her robe and pulled me to a seated position. I wiped my eyes with dirty palms. She pulled a few folded tissues from some invisible pocket. I took them and repaired what damage I could. I shook the dust from the back of my hair and held my hand out. She hauled me up with a vibrant step backward and I followed behind her.

"Are you going to the practice interview?" She asked as she poured hot water into a brown mug. The teabag floated in the water, and she dunked it with a spoon. I shrugged.

"Does that mean you don't know if you're going or that you don't know what it is?"

"Both, I guess."

"Ahhh. I see." I waited for her to go on, but she did not.

"What's a practice interview, then?" I asked with mild irritation. She smiled.

"You'll meet with a teacher who will help you in your practice."

"What practice? Help me how?"

"That's up to you."

"I'm not Buddhist; I don't practice anything."

"Then that is your practice." I looked at her dumbfounded. She smiled, squeezed the teabag into her mug and set it on her saucer. "You know, Vann, a rut is merely a grave with both ends knocked out."

The tea scalded my tongue; I had to drink it slower.

* * *

A small group gathered before an enormous mound of carefully placed wood on top of a stone slab. They chanted and bowed. Each person was allowed to place items on the pyre as a physical representation of nonattachment. The flowers and fruit from the table were taken up one-by-one by teachers and students. His monastic robes were draped on top of that. Leslie asked if Lisa and I would like to place his bowl and cup on the pyre. Lisa stoically lifted the simple wooden bowl and rested it in a bed of flowers. My hands were trembling badly as I reached for the unremarkable cup. I felt an overwhelming need to keep it and looked at the Abiding Teacher for a long time before she nodded me toward the effigy. I set the cup inside the bowl and backed away.

It wasn't until they lit the whole thing on fire that I realized how cold I was. It seemed fitting that it would be our father who would warm me then. Everyone was invited to sit with the body in silence as long as wished. I planted myself in the dirt next to Lisa and put my arm around her shoulder. She leaned her head into my neck and let out a long breath.

My hips and knees were way past aching when I climbed to my feet and started toward our cabin about a half hour later. Most of the people were sitting still, not seemingly affected at all by the stiffness and pain that had settled into my back. I didn't even check my watch before throwing myself in the little camp bed. With all the funk and stain of the day still clinging, I sank into a deep, dreamless sleep.

Chapter 20

From the inky blackness of deep sleep, I heard the slightest ting of a bell. The high-pitched toned pierced deeper into my subconscious, dinging louder. The soft ring brought me fully awake, and I sat up in the darkness. I heard the bell again, moving away, the sound drooping as it dissipated. It was cold. I piled on more clothes and laced up my gym shoes. I heard the soft smack of cabin doors on their frames and shuffling of people gathering outside the great hall. I looked for Lisa, but there was no one.

I tried to blend in with the silent crowd outside the great hall, but all eyes were already on me as I looked through the faces for Lisa. I wanted to ask for her, find out if anyone had seen her. This wasn't my show. It's not that I couldn't talk; I knew if I didn't, all would have a way of revealing itself. If I did speak, I would just feel impatient and silly for not already knowing the answer.

I craned my neck to get a view of where the funeral pyre had been burning through the night, but it was too dark away from the cluster of buildings. One of the students motioned for me to fall in behind the Abiding Teacher. I obeyed and matched her footsteps. She walked impossibly slow, shifting her weight from one foot to the other. It was deliberate, trance-like. I looked behind me and saw the other students following suit, even their hands folded in matching mudras. I laced my fingers in front of me and did my best to keep step. We formed a long, single-file chain stretching across the road stabbing into the darkness.

Approaching the pyre, I heaved a sigh of relief seeing Lisa already there, a quilt draped over her shoulders hanging to the ground. I flooded with worry when I realized she had stayed out there all night. But her face seemed serene and comfortably glowed beside the stone slab. There were a few others nearby watching our approach with relief and gratitude.

When we neared the pile of ashy chunks, the Abiding Teacher paused for a moment until everyone stopped. She bowed deeply, knelt, flattened herself on the ground and unfolded herself up. She silently lifted a metal canister from the base of the stone slab and scooped some of the remains. She turned from the altar and started walking slowly into the darkness.

I watched as the others who had stayed through the night, prostrated before the slab, scooped the ashes of my father and moved slowly into the breaking dawn. It was such a simple gesture and so profoundly loving, I could barely understand what I was seeing. Lisa stepped in front of me and took her turn.

A few in the line moved past me, repeating the steps and connecting the line. Linda, the director, stepped from behind the stone slab and brought me an empty metal container where I stood. She bowed, picked up a container for herself, filled it and filed in line. The person behind me waited. I bowed over gingerly and took my can to the altar. There were recognizable chunks of wood and human bone, some still glowing with heat. I dipped my can into the remains and shuttled myself in the direction the others had gone.

The ashes and embers were warm in my hands. I tucked it closer into my body, realizing I was holding my dad. And somehow, he was holding me.

The slightest rays of the sun peaked through the eastern valley graying the black shadows of early dawn. We followed a trail away from the center past a rock formation that looked like hands folded in prayer. I stopped to take it in fully but moved along when I heard the next person nearing me from behind.

The trail ended at a memorial to Shunryu Suzuki Roshi, the founder of the San Francisco Zen Center from which Tassajara was formed. There were stones and monuments to other Zen Masters along the edge of the trail nearby. The sun swaddled the trail by the time all of us gathered.

"Nelson Mandela said there is nothing like returning to a place that remains unchanged to find the ways in which you yourself have altered," Leslie said clearly over the wind careening across the top of the mountain. "As we return our brother Timothy to the earth in his altered form, recall how you yourself have changed because of his time in this place and in your life."

She turned away from the group and walked just past the memorial. We all watched her as she pulled her container of my father's ashes back then pushed them wide into the wind. She came back through the crowd and moved toward the return trail. As she passed me, her eyes were low and loosely focused on the trail in front of her feet. The warming rays of sun washed over her face, glistening with fresh tears.

His friends and family took turns lofting Dad's ashes onto the mountain. The wind picked them up and he sailed out over the valley as far as I could see. Seeing the grey powder swirl in the shifting gusts brought a memory back like the prick of a safety pin.

Our game. Just Dad and me. He would take me by the hands and twirl until my feet left the ground. My heart leapt. I could see my little sundress flapping and Dad's house shoes clapping against the kitchen floor as if I was right that very moment the same little girl I had always been. Dad had not left my mom who had not become an intolerable drunk. His face was split wide with a smile of delight. And I knew without out a doubt, no matter what happened next and after that, he loved me. In his own way, as best he could, he loved me this whole time. I had just forgotten how to be that little barefoot girl, squealing with thrill, never afraid he would let go or hurt me.

I felt the inertia of spinning in the breeze push through my hair on the mountain. I stumbled away from the cluster of mourners, away from the trail, away from the betrayal, hurt and indignation, away from the shitty things I had become. I took the remains of my father and twirled in a circle, spinning the ashes in a wide circle that blew back in my clothes, hair and tears. I sat down, sobbing, completely surrounded in a ring of Dad. Clutching the empty container like I would never let go, I cried myself out.

A while after the shuffling of feet against rock and the whooshing of ashes against cool air had stopped, I stood up and smiled weakly over the vast expanse of the valley stretched endlessly before me.

"Goodbye, Daddy," I said to the sun and the wind and tears and pain. "I love you."

Lisa waited for me back on the road. I had nearly forgotten she had come, but when I saw her, I flooded with warmth. We hugged for a long time.

"I'm glad we came," she said.

"Me too." We crossed the road to our cabin to start packing up the few things we had a chance to use while we were there. It had been less than a day but felt like an eternity.

"How was your practice interview?" she asked me.

"I haven't done one." I said confused.

"You didn't?"

"You did?"

"Yes, last night while Dad was…finishing up. Are you not going to do it?"

"I hadn't thought about it, really. I guess I thought someone would ask me when it was time. I had tea with the director last night. That doesn't count?"

"Do you want to take your interview now?"

"I still don't even know what they are."

"No problem; it's best really."

"Now you sound all cryptic like the people here."

"It's only cryptic if you aren't ready for the message."

"Thanks for making my point. What does that even mean?" She laughed at me.

"It means you weren't ready for the message. Go see if you can find one of the teachers and ask if they have time for the interview."

"What, just go up to them and ask 'can you be a buddy and confuse me some more?'"

"I'll get the truck ready." She jerked her head toward the door, gesturing for me to get going.

I knocked softly on the director's cabin door. She met my eyes and held it open for me to come inside.

"Hey, Linda. Thank you and everyone for everything. It was really moving. I mean, I felt moved."

"Good, I'm glad. Are you all leaving now?"

"Well, actually, Lisa said I should do that practice interview before we left." My tone turned up at the end like I was asking a question.

"She did, did she? Do you want to interview?"

"I guess. Well, I have some questions, but I'd like to do it, yes."

"During a practice interview, the questions are for you."

"So, that doesn't really make a lot of sense to me. No one has really told me what it is or the purpose or anything. I thought maybe it was supposed to help me understand what happened here, maybe. But I don't know what to expect."

"Ahh, yes. Then don't expect anything. Then you won't set yourself up to be let down." She laughed to herself, but I wasn't in on the joke. Seeing my discomfort, she put a long firm arm around my shoulder. "Wait here. I'll see if Leslie can see you now."

She glided to the door and put on her sandals. I looked down at my feet realizing I had forgotten to take off my shoes. It felt silly because I knew I was about to put them back on, but I unlaced them and set them on the rack outside her door.

She returned quickly and I met her at the doorway.

"It looks like Leslie is attending other matters."

"Can you do an interview?" I cut her off.

"I don't usually...but I suppose I could."

"Oh, that would be great. Thank you so much."

"Sounds like you've decided you do want to do a practice interview."

"I guess so." We were both smiling.

"Follow me. There's a small meditation room off the yoga lodge we can use." I followed her trying to sort out my questions and expectations on the short walk.

The room was small, like a closet. There were two cushions on pads and a small altar on what looked like an overgrown footstool. There was a mini statue of the Buddha with three tea lights along with a small bowl of sand and a small bowl of water. I wondered if Buddhists get baptized like

Christians or what other use there would be for the water. Linda gestured for me to sit on the cushion across from her. I sat cross-legged and watched as she lit the candles with a match. She pulled a stick of incense from behind the statue and lit it from the candle on the right. She put it out by waving it in the air and then poked it into the bowl of sand so that it stood straight up sending a string of smoke skyward.

She gathered her robes and lowered herself onto the cushion. Once she settled, the hem of her robes completely enveloped the cushion making it look like she was levitating above the floor. It was simple and magical at the same. She closed her eyes and took in a few deep breaths. I closed my eyes and tried to follow along matching my breathing to hers and sitting up straighter.

Finally, she opened her eyes and looked warmly at me, a small smile fixed. She looked at me fully, with her whole body and mind. I could feel her completely connected to me. It was uncomfortable to feel exposed in that way but soothing to be wholly present at the same time.

"Vann, I know you have questions, and you must discover which is the right one." I took a breath like I was going to start blabbing but stopped when I realized what she said. The right one? Just one? How is there just one right question? Realizing I had created a dozen more questions, I paused to still my swirling thoughts. I looked at her as if she would go on, but she waited for me to actually ask one right question. I felt awkward and intensely curious. How was I going to know which was the right one? It seemed entirely ludicrous.

I wanted to know how I had gotten so far from who I thought I was and who I wanted to be? How was I so heart-broken by losing my father whom I had barely known? How did I suddenly feel like I had known him all this time but was veiled by perceived abandonment? I had been the one who exited myself from his life, hadn't I? I wanted to know what all this meant. More specifically, could I forgive my father? I felt certain I had forgiven him already, maybe even just this morning, but could I forgive myself? Was that the right question?

It already seemed like I had sat there for a day or two, mouth open, but not speaking. Linda was actively conjuring up truth from my very bewildered consciousness.

"Honestly," I started with apprehension. "I've never felt closer to Dad than I do now. I feel like I understand him, know him in a way that would never have been possible if he..." I looked at her for affirmation. She nodded but did not interrupt.

"I also learned some things about myself and my own perceptions that make me feel lost and saddened by the person I've become." I paused again, wishing she would help me out. She smiled; she nodded; she expressed every warmth but would not interrupt. Realizing I had not yet asked any question, I took a deep breath and tried to distill it to the right one.

"My right question is..." I felt certain I could not go on. Whatever I would say couldn't possibly be the right question. In a flash of non-thinking, non-expectations, I finally asked, "How do I get home?"

It sounded so stupid, but I knew there could be no other question. Linda's already-wide smile broadened impossibly further. I heaved out a sigh of relief releasing years of anxiety. I almost laughed. It was the right question. How do I get home? I was euphoric. I didn't even care what the answer was; I just knew I had to get back to my authentic self somehow. I could see Linda watching all this play out on my face. She was experiencing the release with me. We hung there in a silent celebration.

When the moment passed, she closed her eyes and took a few slow, rhythmic breaths. I realized she was going to answer my question. I hadn't expected there to be an answer coming and felt jarred. I righted my posture and tried to bring myself fully present in the moment.

"Jetsun Milarepa, the Tibetan yogi and poet, had searched everywhere for enlightenment—for the answer to his question. Finally, one day, he saw an old man walking slowly down a mountain path carrying a heavy sack over his shoulder." Linda mimed holding a bag over her shoulder, straining against its weight. "Sensing this old man knew the answer to his question he stopped him and said 'Old man, please tell me what you know. How do I obtain enlightenment?' The old man smiled at him for a moment then slung the heavy burden from over his shoulder laying it aside and stood straight." She gestured putting down a sack next to her and straightened on her cushion.

She continued, "'Yes, I see!' cried Milarepa who was instantly enlightened. After thanking the old man for his deep wisdom, Milarepa said, 'But please, one more question you must answer for me. What is after enlightenment?' Smiling at him again, the old wise man picked up his load, steadied himself and continued on his way." She hefted the imaginary sack over her shoulder again and leaned forward against its weight.

I didn't have to ask, I understood immediately. The whole truth came rushing in. I had lugged around a heavy burden of hurt and bitterness for most of my life. And it didn't matter what was in the load: my anger toward my dad or toward myself.

Being at Tassajara, I had experienced what it felt like to finally lay down the full weight of my troubles. It's always a shock to your system when you stop fighting and give way to flow. Not knowing what to do with nothing to carry, my system had revolted, turned on itself. I didn't see anything past the sack on the ground. I started at it, going 'look at all the shit in that bag'! I couldn't go any further and I certainly couldn't go back.

How do I get home? I pick up the sack and walk on. It seemed so simple and so sacred, I couldn't believe I didn't always know the answer. It was my load, my life; there's no leaving it behind, going on without it or magically transforming into something else. I carry it all with me, but it's just a sack. I make it a burden, I lay it down. I see it for what it is, pick it up and go on. It was my flash flood enlightenment.

I bowed over so deeply on my cushion, my forehead nearly touched the floor. After I had sat up, she bowed to me. We stood up and I hugged her hard.

"Thank you. Thank you for that," I said with my chin dug into her shoulder.

"You're most welcome, Vann. But don't misunderstand." She held me by the shoulders at arm's length looking me in the eye. "You found the question. And you found the answer." I nodded meekly. I didn't want the responsibility of being my own savior but knew there was none other. "Now, go, be home."

Chapter 21

We drove straight through on the way home. I
didn't dread the descent from the mountain; it was
part of the journey. I let Lisa drive that first leg
though. We should have been impossibly tired and
foul, not rejuvenated and bubbling. We laughed
and shared our very different experiences, like we
had just come from a carnival: I had been in the fun
house while she was on the roller coaster.

I hadn't felt such levity and wholeness since we
were girls. We promised each other to hang onto
that feeling as long as we could, to be closer and not
lose the secrets Tassajara Zen Mountain Center
have given up to us.

Back in Vancouver, I hugged my mom
voraciously on sight. She was flabbergasted but
grateful. We ate mom's fried chicken dinner with
crazy sweet tea as a family. We traded stories of
what the girls and Mike had done while we were
gone and of our adventures. We left some of our
adventures out, Lisa and I exchanging nervous
glances as we tip-toed around our timeline gaps.

After convincing Mike to spend one more night
alone with the girls, Lisa and I piled up in bed on
either side of Mom and giggled ourselves to sleep.

My flight home was early. I crept out of the
house not wanting to wake anyone and not wanting
to leave. The cab waited to ferry me back to PDX.
Before I boarded, Lisa sent me a text: Have a great

trip. Miss you already! XOXO. I sent her a winky face and put my phone in airplane mode. I smiled to myself realizing I had spent the whole time at Tassajara in airplane mode. I had been disconnected, but completely grounded. A funny, magical place with a great window-to-the-soul seat.

* * *

On the way to his apartment, I hadn't thought about what I would say to Daisuke. There was so much to tell him and not much to talk about at the same time. I anticipated the strength in his arms when he hugged me. I wondered if he would notice anything different about me—a softened strength I had mystically acquired on my trip.

I slipped my key to his apartment in the lock and turned it. The door pushed open, already unlocked.

"Dai! I'm back!" I called into the living room. I hung my purse over the chair in the foyer where his keys and wallet lay as usual. "Sorry I didn't get a chance to call. I just got in..." I said as I rounded to corner into the living room where I could see his back sitting on a stool at the kitchen bar. I felt a rush of warmth, familiar and missed. At least until he jerked around at the sound of my voice, and I saw the utter look of shock on what was actually Maru's face.

I was immediately immersed in water: not breathing, not hearing, unable to speak. Maru and I blinked wildly at each other. I went completely blank. I couldn't form thoughts or words or vocalization. The sky had ripped open, and aliens took over.

Daisuke, who had been leaning on the fridge, came at me with his arms outstretched. I must have stumbled backward unless the couch bumped into me.

"Vann?" she said first, eyes locked on mine. I mouthed her name. Daisuke had one hand on my back, propping me up.

"Funny thing," he said to Maru. "She came here when she couldn't find you." I looked at him and back at her. My mouth open, eyes wide. Funny thing? More like fucking ridiculous and bizarrely ironic. Maru's eyes bounced from me to her brother to his familiar and gentle hand supporting the low curve of my back.

She knew. I saw it when it registered on her face. I had never met him when she left. Now I had my own key to his apartment, and it was the first place I came when I got back from travelling home. Now his hand was on my back, and I was leaning into him. She knew. The look of shock on her face turned dark and her jaw clenched.

The three of us stood motionless like that for almost ever, but maybe just a few extremely uncomfortable seconds. Any guilt I had initially felt steamed off during the silent stretch while I converted to pure disgust. Fury like you get when you're looking for someone for three months and they show up not dead, not hurt, not different in any way. Maru held my stark-mad gaze and finally looked away.

I stepped carefully up to her as if she were a fine statue. Honestly, I didn't know if I was going to hit her or kiss her. It just seemed too unreal. Maru. Sitting here in Daisuke's apartment. Not with me. Or was I not with her? The complex swirl of thought continued to twist, almost visible in the air.

"I was just telling her your father died last week," Daisuke said.

"Is that all?" I asked him while glaring at her. His silence said he hadn't told her anything about us or of any actual value in sorting out our shit show.

"So, you didn't tell her that I felt like dying when she left me? You didn't mention the missing person's report I almost filed or the scene I made at the coffee shop when I found out she had told you but not me that she was leaving L.A.?"

"No." He said so softly that he shouldn't have bothered.

"Did you know?" I finally asked her. "Did you know what you did to me? Did you see my messages? Know I completely fell apart?" She wouldn't look at me but shook her head. "How did you think this would play out? You, what, would just come home and I would be just the way you left me?" If I could have helped it, I would have stopped the tears. Instead, my emotions welled up violently and spilled out over my cheeks.

"I thought...I thought you would die before you would have done that to me," I said, my voice shaking. "I never thought you of all people, you. Maru, you know me. You couldn't have not known..." My voice eked out in a strained, flat line.

The rest of the universe blanked out in the backdrop as I honed all my hurt and anger and betrayal and fear at her.

"Vann, I..." she reached for me, but I pulled my arm away.

"No, Maru. You don't get to just...no. I don't want to miss the way your hands feel on me ever again."

"I'm sorry, Vann," she said, her voice deeper than I remembered. An internal trigger soothed me by the mellow warmth of her voice. "I just needed to...regroup."

"Regroup? Are you serious?"

"It's not that simple."

"Oh, I think it was. I think it was too simple for you to leave your whole life behind, your car, your phone, your own wallet, Maru. What did you think I was going to think?" I nearly shouted at her.

"Vann, I need to talk to you about this—"

"Then speak!" She glanced over at Daisuke.

"No, he stays. He needs to hear this too. I wasn't the only one you left."

"It's ok, Vann," Daisuke said. "You two can talk alone—"

"No! Both of you. If have something to say to me, Maru, you say it to him too."

"So, what, are you two best friends now?"

"You know what we are," I said tersely. Maru glanced at who Daisuke looked like he wanted to crawl in the cabinets and hide. Big ugly truths always have a way of making me want to avert the blow. But there was no way she didn't know or that I was going to try to hide the obvious.

"Are you sleeping with her?" she asked.

"Maru, you—" he started, but didn't need to finish. He nodded and hung his head to his chest. She looked back at me, tears trembling in her eyes. I tried to remember any time I'd seen her cry but couldn't. It sent pangs through my chest to see her hurting but just as much as my own hurting felt like the wings of a great bird against a cage.

"I tried to find you," I said finally. "I thought you were dead. I thought you were dead. As in, there was no other explanation for what could have happened."

"When you said you were leaving L.A., I never imagined you didn't tell your own wife," he said.

"My wife," she fired at him like shotgun spray. "My wife."

"You don't get to be all dejected here, Maru." I said, stepping into her line of view. "You left your wife, remember. What did you think was going to happen when you just didn't come home?"

"I don't know. I didn't think you'd start fucking my brother." It was her words that shot this time. She didn't use those kinds of words, ever. The air thickened on contact with nastiness spit out.

"Yeah, and I never thought you'd up and vanish like you never loved me at all. I guess we both had a lot to learn about the person we married."

"Hmph. You think I never loved you?"

"When you love someone, you don't trick them like that and just leave? Did you read my messages to you? I thought I was suffocating, completely crazy!"

"I said it's complicated."

"So is the whole thing with Daisuke, so leave your condescension at the door."

"Vann," he said with such tenderness in his voice, it reminded me of how he called my name when we made love. "Before you go on, you'll want to listen to her."

I looked at him searching for answers in the unspoken code we shared but only found sincerity in his warning. "What does that mean? What does he mean, Maru?"

She wiped her eyes with her palms and took a pained breath. "He means why I had to leave."

"I hardly think you had to leave. But yes, I'd love to hear this. I've wanted to hear nothing else for months. Please—"

"Vann, hear her." It was slow and deliberate the way his words had calmed me in the past months of utter turmoil. I took a breath and turned to her. I could see on her face the mixture of pain and intrigue about the connection and response I had with her brother. It was nothing like the lop-sided communication we had shared and I'm sure it stung. In some ways she was meeting us both for the first time. Daisuke and I had a bond, not her.

"I do want to know. I want to know so badly, I'm shaking inside and out, Maru. Please tell me what happened that drove you hurt me so deeply?" Daisuke shot me a 'leave it' look and I brushed him off.

"I can't believe that you—" Anticipating another admonishment about an affair, I folded my arms and prepared to unload a dump truck of bitterness on her. "—you could think I didn't love you."

It was unexpected. I didn't know how to respond, but it wasn't what I had wanted to know. Besides, I did know, or at least believed that she loved me. I wasn't sure how it was possible to love someone and up-and-disappear like that at the same time. "How do you—" I started

"Vann," Daisuke interrupted. "You need to know."

"Need to know what? What is it?" I was angry and irritated beyond rationality and in no mood to dance.

"Cancer," she said.

I didn't register the correlation at first. I thought 'cancer what'? I do remember the seething anger and carved hurt flushed immediately from my system just as quickly as it had rushed to the surface. Confusion, chaos and questions replaced every molecule bouncing around in and around me.

"It's cancer, Vann. I didn't know for sure..." I stepped over to her and instinctively took both her hands in mine. I don't know if I was just suffering from rapid-onset shock or just overwhelmed with emotion. I squatted in front of her, squeezing her hands hard, looking down in disbelief. The breath I took was very audible and even surprised me.

"Why would you not tell me? Me?" I shook my head at the floor as tears splattered the linoleum. "Why would you not come to me instead of run away?" I looked up at her, my eyes flicking back and forth at hers. "Ru," I whispered, squeezing tighter. "Why all this?"

We hung there in time and space. Her sitting on the stool, me on my knees at her feet, Daisuke leaning over the counter. Her and then him, and then Dad, then Alex and Tassajara just welled up and washed over me taking all the attention I had left to pay the universe, and I just hung out there. No words, no thoughts, no knowing. Coveted emptiness, because nothing remained taking up space in my consciousness.

It could have been days later when she finally touched me on the shoulder. I didn't even know if it was her or him. Just blank.

"I didn't do it right, I know." I heard her say. I couldn't lock my brain around what it meant or what I thought. But maybe that's what truly listening to someone really is. No judgments or reply, just the words on a blank canvas in your presence.

"I know now I should have told you. I thought I was protecting you."

"How did you think that was protecting her?" Daisuke asked. She paused a long time before answering.

"I'm not going to fight it," she said.

"What do you mean? It's curable right? There's a chance," he said.

"Yes," she hesitated.

"But what?"

"But nothing. The drugs and treatments are nasty, and I didn't want to go through it, and I didn't want to put her through that either. Or you. Or Mom and Dad."

"Why now?" I heard myself say from the floor. The sound of my own voice shuttled me back from desolation. I rose slowly and hefted myself onto the barstool across from her.

"You can get stomach cancer at any age. We have a history of it in my family. Well, in our entire race, really."

"No, why did you come back now? If you slunk off like a cat to die alone, why are you here now, with this?"

"I don't know."

"You don't know?" Daisuke asked.

"She knows, don't you?" I said soaking tears from my eyes with the hem of my shirt. She was still so familiar to me; I had known her inside and out as much as anyone could, as much as she would let me. But I felt her move in me, underneath the bullshit and pain. After everything fell apart, I understood her unspoken need.

"I was going to Canada where they, you know, they have assisted..." She couldn't even say it. Suicide is scornful in Japanese culture. She knew it would mean betraying her family and heritage. It was so reprehensible, she couldn't say the word. "I mean, I went to the airport and took a cab to our apartment and..." she hesitated for a long time, but I knew.

I stepped in close between her legs where she sat and slid my arms behind her back. Pulling her into me with too much force, I felt the full figure of her body press against mine. It was desperation more than loving. I pressed my cheek to hers and whispered tersely into her ear, "You were never alone." I felt her arms engage around me and her breathing me in, my smell and warmth and sweetness. "You didn't have to be scared; I would have loved you through it."

I pulled away, my hands on her shoulders. She looked past me, sorting through fears and regrets.

"I messed up. Terribly." I nodded and stepped back farther. "I'm so sorry."

"Oh God, Maru, I am too," I said, resigning. "I still love you; I'll always love you. How could you not have known that?"

"I thought...I don't know what I thought."

"Seems like you didn't think very much," Daisuke said. Her glance was wounded.

"Once they told me for sure, I just wanted to get out, get away. The options are—ugly. I don't want that. I don't. That's what I know."

"Whatever made you come home instead of going to the airport, thank you," I said. "I don't know if I would have ever recovered if I never knew what happened."

"So, you were going to Canada because assisted suicide is legal there?" Daisuke asked. She nodded. I could tell there was something darkly Japanese going on there. He looked disgusted and she soaked with shame.

"There's nothing wrong with dying with dignity," I said to diffuse them. "I don't like it. You don't have to like it, Dai. But it's her choice."

"Why do you call him that?" she asked.

"Call him what?"

"Dai, like Die."

"His name is really long, I guess. Like I call you Ru."

"I thought you called me that because...because it's how you love me."

"It is, I guess. A term of endearment."

"So?" I glanced over at Daisuke for a bailout. I knew what she was asking, but he seemed lost.

"Yes," I said. "I love him." I kept my eyes on her, but knew he was looking heavily at me. When I glanced up at him, the chocolate in his eyes melted all over me. I hadn't told him I loved him before. It was like having an extremely intimate conversation through an interpreter. I saw her watching this exchange and braced for her reaction.

And slowly, the strangest thing happened. Her face softened as she resigned to the idea. It was nearly audible. She sat there, forcing herself be ok with us. She looked back and forth between us, knitting us together with her eyes. With a deep breath, she nodded. It was then I saw her, truly her. She wanted me to be happy. Badly managed and mangled up to this point, I knew she was packing up her pain to prevent my own.

"I imagined this moment a thousand times," I finally said. "What I would say to you; what I would do to you. It never came out like this."

"Me too," she laughed a little and I followed suit. "None of this." Daisuke came around the bar and hugged us both. She buried her face in his shoulder. My mind swirled and buzzed. It was a soap opera culminating in the kitchen, right there in a huge hole in my life.

Chapter 22

The three of us piled on Daisuke's typical-male leather couch with stiff drinks and broken-open hearts. While they discussed the particulars of her escapades and ultimate request, I watched them entranced. I could barely separate them in my senses and on my body. They were talking about breaking it to their mom and dad while I was thinking there was no way I could be with him and not think of her. No way his hands on me would not feel just like hers in the dark. I knew all this about her already: she wanted to be cremated; she wanted the ashes spread at home, in Japan home. She had always said her brother should do it. He was "her brother" until he became Daisuke. Dai. A man who I apparently loved and by which I was profoundly puzzled. Daisuke should spread her ashes. Not me. I could not love her enough to earn that right.

I couldn't help but think of spreading my father's ashes in a wide circle, flakes still warm sticking to my tear-streaked face. I hadn't loved my father enough to earn the right to spread his ashes either. As much as I may have fought for the privilege before, I knew I didn't want to be the one to carry out her final wishes. I couldn't take another knife in the gut like that.

I looked at their faces. Daisuke cried; Maru tried to soothe him.

My father's ashes. Her ashes. My lover. Who? Tassajara; Lisa, sweet Lisa, what happened in San Francisco? What happened to me? What was Alex? What am I now? Questions rushed up like the rising waters of a swift river under an overturned canoe. My whole world was sitting right here in this room and was about to be completely gone. What did that make me? I felt guilty and gross. About to slip under water, I blurted out, "I slept with Alex!"

They both looked over from their very intense, very intimate conversation and asked "Who?" in unison.

"In San Francisco. Lisa and I went to a bar on the way to dad's funeral. And she left and I stayed and—"

"Who is Alex?" Daisuke asked firmly, but the dam had broken and it poured out.

"I feel so terrible and this whole situation. I hadn't heard from you; I didn't know what to do and now I feel so guilty, and I just want you to know. I don't even know what happened; it just happened—"

"Vann, Vann. Stop, Vann," he tried again. My mouth was still open, ready for more, but I halted suddenly realizing what I had done. Maru looked at me with wild eyes. I could see on her face, she didn't know me anymore. I remember thinking I didn't know me anymore either. The whole situation. It was all over the place; I was all over the place.

"What are you talking about?" Dai asked.

"My dad's funeral. Well, not his funeral, but on the way there."

"Ok, and what happened?" Maru was struck silent; her head tilted like she was trying to hear me better because she couldn't believe what I was saying.

"Why are you looking at me like that?" I asked her.

"What happened, Vann?" Dai cut in again. The rims of his eyes were red, and his voice was near breaking. I remember wishing I hadn't said anything. That this wasn't going to end well. I shouldn't have piled on; this wasn't the time or place. But just as quickly that there was no time and place for any of this whole mess. Wasn't I a victim somewhere in here? Am I not entitled to royal fuck ups?

"I don't know why I brought it up," I said taking a breath. "I'm sorry I said anything."

"You brought it up, Vann. I don't know why either, why now, but you did."

"I guess I just feel so overwhelmed, and I thought we were getting things off our chests here."

"Ok," he said, considering it. "Get it off your chest. What happened on the way to Tassajara?"

"I'm not really sure. Well, I mean, I know what happened. But I don't know what happened to me."

"Did you know him? Was he just some stranger in a bar?"

"She," Maru said so softly, it was like a leaf flittering in a rainstorm of conversation.

"She?" Daisuke seemed confused. I nodded and the dumbfounded look was on his face now.

"Vann is gay," she said.

"That's not fair, Maru. You don't get to decide that."

"But you are," she said louder. I flicked my eyes toward Daisuke who went rigid on the couch, eyes hurting.

"I don't know what I am," my leaf flittered into the rainstorm. "I didn't think it mattered." But it did matter; I could tell it mattered to him, at least. I looked down at my hands trembling in my lap. "I don't know what it means. I don't know what any of this means. I just thought you should know."

"Know what?" Daisuke said, his voice crackled from his thickened throat.

"None of us are perfect here," I said. "This whole situation is..." He looked away, and Maru and I both knew he was the only one getting hurt who didn't deserve it. There was nothing I could say. I reached for his hand, his warm wonderful hand that had been so strong for me these past months. It was rigid and unresponsive on his knee. Maru's gaze met mine with icy Japanese scorn, and I snapped my hand back.

"I'm sorry you were hurt," I said to him. "But I'm not sorry it happened." I couldn't believe the words I was saying, or that he nodded. What did that mean? I felt a tug in my gut toward San Francisco chased by the pang of confusion in the room. "I learned some things about myself while I was gone. A lot really. And I'm glad for everything that happened. The fight with my mom, the breakthrough with my sister, the heartbreak with my father. Alex. Everything."

"I'm glad you told me," he said. "I know it must have been...hard for you."

"Which part?" I asked.

"All of it. For all of us." An then we were all nodding. Not like everything was ok, nodding. But like, this is just how it ends sometimes, nodding.

I remember thinking what is the right thing to do for her and for me. And for Daisuke. Is there even an answer to a question like that? I felt like I was rushing the streets of L.A. again looking for my lost lover, lost all over again. But there was no harried panic, just the pain of searching, of not knowing. I felt like I was just slipping away into my life without either of them.

* * *

Daisuke followed us back to our apartment where I had not been in what felt like years. And Grover acted like it too. He hopped all over Maru and peed with excitement. She knelt down and let him lick her face with serious gusto.

I saw the box of her things where I had left them in the hall. After sleeping with Daisuke, they had nowhere to go and were just hanging out until she got home. She didn't look in the box. But it looked at me.

After a lousy pizza and two solid bottles of wine, the three of us shared some awkward looks about sleeping arrangements. Daisuke was quick to throw himself on the couch and proclaim he "would just crash here." Maru hesitated, but then rescinded. There was no easy way to iron it out, but I could tell she was exhausted and wanted to sleep in her own bed.

"Go ahead and lay down," I said. "I'll be right there. We can talk if you want." She nodded and disappeared into the blackness of our bedroom. I heard the door to the bathroom click shut and turned to Daisuke.

"You ok?" I asked sitting on the coffee table in front of the couch. He shook his head and reached for my hip, pulling me closer to him. He sank his face in my lap.

"I'm so...tired," he said into my thighs. I rubbed my palms into his back feeling the warmth and broadness of him.

"I know, it's been a long day."

"It's been a long life," he said throwing himself into the back of the couch.

"No kidding."

"I have to take my sister to Canada." His face was a lost little boy's. "How am I supposed to do that?"

"The same way you do anything. The same way I said goodbye to a man I barely know. You just do. And it hurts when it hits you in the face; but you just do it." He was quiet for a moment thinking this over.

"I feel like I've already lost you," he said looking up at me. A rush of tears sprang up in my eyes. I instinctively wiped them away before he might notice, but too late. "It's true, isn't it?"

I nodded. "It's true I love you—" I broke off.

"I love you too, Vann," he said pleading. I covered my mouth with a shaking hand. He pulled away from my face toward his. I felt the smooth sweetness of his caramel skin. "It's ok," he whispered.

"It's not," I shook my head. "I can't be with you without thinking of her, Dai."

"You don't have to. You don't have to not think about her."

"No, Dai. I can't feel you without feeling her. Do you understand?" He looked at me, searching. "I can't smell you, can't see you, can't...I just can't." I pulled my hand back to wipe away the relentless tears.

"Don't you think this all happened for a reason? Does it mean something?"

"I think it means love is all fucked up." I looked over my shoulder to the bedroom.

"Don't say that. Don't just blow this off because you don't want to feel anything."

"Feel anything? I feel everything. That's the problem. What about the whole Alex thing, what about what she said about me being gay?"

"Maru said a lot of things about you. They're not all true, are they?"

"I don't know. What all did she say?"

He fluttered his eyes and said, "I don't care about Alex. You don't care about Alex. It doesn't mean anything."

"It doesn't mean anything to you. What about what it means to me?"

"You said you don't know what it means. That's what it means."

"That makes no sense. I can't believe we're having this conversation right now. Your sister is in the next room."

"Were you ever going to have this conversation with me? Why not now."

"Dai, Maru, your sister, is in the bedroom. It's not like she can't hear us. Are you kidding me?"

"So, so what. You just waive us off and that's it?"

"How did you think this was going to end?"

"I didn't think about ending, Vann. I thought about never being in love before. Never feeling like my own person with my own heart beating in my chest until I fell for you. So no, I didn't think about how it was going to end."

I sat next to him on the couch. "You never talked to me about how you felt. Why are you just now telling me?"

"I didn't think I had to tell you. I thought you felt like I do. You don't feel it here?" he asked pressing his palm to my chest. I clasped my hand around his and nodded, crying all over again.

I remember not wanting to feel heartsick, not wanting to feel anything. Not wanting to feel the pangs of longing that come with love and, eventually, loss. But it was all there. I hadn't said it before today, but I knew it was true. I had fallen for him. It was so casual, I barely noticed. That giddy little girl that had played around in my head had planned out a beautiful life of us together.

I sat there across from him, again feeling fully taken in and still saddened by who I had become. My question lolled at the base of my brain and stung when it came to the front: Was he my home? Was I supposed to stop fighting it?

I brought his fingers to my lips and kissed them. "I have to go to her," I said avoiding his eyes.

"Vann," he whispered. I was already moving around the coffee table away from him. "Vann," he called louder as I slipped into the darkened doorway of the bedroom.

I slipped between the covers and folded myself over Maru just as I had done 3,000 times before. I felt her arm wrap around my back and her heavy sigh.

"What are you going to do?" she asked. I knew what she was asking but had no answer whether or not I was supposed to give one. I was quiet for a moment.

"I'm going to hold you tonight." She pulled me tighter into her.

Of all the scenarios I imagined that might play out should I ever see her again, this was not one. How do you see something like this? Any of this? With two lovers in one tiny apartment, I felt torn in half. It wasn't guilt, just raw, exposed nerves. And maybe I had done a fine job for most of my life up to that point of armoring myself against feeling any real emotion. But I could tell Tassajara had split me wide, shattering those over-crusted defenses. In a way, it was the best gift my father could have given me. All those years ago, it was he who first taught me heartbreak, bitterness and the corresponding self-preservation tactics that had served me well, keeping anyone I loved at arm's length. Now, it was he who had given me the chance to see things, see myself, as I truly am. And to let it go.

I would have to let her go, again. I would have to let him go too. But right then, I would just lay there and be comfort to her. Allow myself to feel wretched euphoria or whatever came in. The right question was, am I home?

The answer? I knew I would always love her, love who we had been. But lying there in the dark, my eyes closed and wet, her hands pressing into my back and breath in my hair felt just like his.

Chapter 23

I would say I woke up if I was sure I had fallen asleep at all. I was tired in my bones, brought all the way down to the nub. But there's no sleeping through thoughts like wild horses.

When Maru sucked in a waking gasp and found my eyes, I was awake, quite awake, and looking directly at her. She reached for my hip under the sheets and squeezed. The burning, swirling memory of our last morning together came rushing in.

"Everything ok?" she asked, but I didn't have to wonder how long she had been watching. All night. About to make the biggest, hardest and worst decision she would ever have trouncing her sleep.

I dashed half a smile but did not reply. I laced my fingers through her hand on my hip, pulled them above the covers and brushed my lips over her knuckles. As much as our last mornings together were identical, we were rearranged women now. I wouldn't fake a stretch and make her breakfast. I would stay there with her and lay in the pain of what was coming next.

Puffy eyed Daisuke made us breakfast that looked like lunch: steamed rice, miso soup and pan-seared tofu. There was no use in trying to outcook Maru, so he went with their traditional home breakfast for comfort. Maru smiled from the side of her mouth at the sight of the spread. Daisuke nodded.

I watched their coded body language as an intruder. Daisuke had made three servings, but I was acutely aware that I should not be there. Maru had chosen him to comfort her in the end for good reason. He knew without asking.

"I'm going to shower and do some laundry," I said. They looked up from their bowls and blinked at me as if I had just said I pulled up a tree with my bare hands. It was a disbelieving and unconcerned stare.

"Do you know when you plan to tell your parents?"

They looked at each other making a decision I couldn't know. Daisuke cleared his throat and stood up as if a lady entered the room.

"Probably today. If you still want, Maru."

"And then?" I turned to her. She nodded her reply.

Daisuke's hand on the back of his chair, Maru slouched motionless over her trio of bowls, I stared at my twin lovers. I would never be able to feel them apart. Whatever love I felt for him would be no salve for the pain I felt in losing her.

When I brushed past him to the bedroom—the place where we had first collided in mutual angst—Dai dropped his head, not reaching for me. I looked back to see him accepting me walk away.

I washed the Tassajara sand from my feet, none of it sitting right with me. I tried to picture myself waiting for Daisuke to return from Canada. Would I hug him as he put the ornate box of my wife's ashes on our fireplace mantle? Would we make love in the bed where I had been holding her? Even in a different bed, he was still her in my subconscious' dialect of the flesh. If I closed my eyes when we kissed, would I always be haunted by her?

There was no perfect choice. There was heartbreak either way. And the inertia of a new fold in the path calling.

* * *

"You've got Alex," she said into the phone. The charm of her smooth Southern voice rushing back to and over me.

"Do I?" I was playful.

"Who is this?" I heard her stop shuffling.

"This is your novelty lay who fell for you."

"Vann Townsend." Her voice brightened. Without seeing her, I could tell she was smiling. I felt a tingle of relief that she remembered my name, hell, that she got the answer right at all. "You're calling me back!"

"Well, actually, Alex, you're the one calling me back."

"How's that, darlin'?" Now I was smiling.

"One night wasn't enough, I guess."

"I've got the next, oh, hundred or so free—if you want them." I realized I was holding my breath when I heard she had stopped breathing too. The thrill of mutual feelings buzzed. I covered my mouth to keep from giggling. I wanted to play it cool, but never was.

"I guess I should see if I can get a pet sitter for my dog and cat."

"Nah," she said, and took a slurp of coffee. "Bring them with you and we'll call it a family."

Finally, I was going home.

Other S.E. Chandler Books

Rise & Converge Series

The Lie That Binds

A first-crush kiss chased by a punch in the mouth.

Ehra Havel is pretending to live like the elitist Omeo class that is trying to exploit and extinguish unmatched people just like her. Adopted from the streets of futuristic Chicago by an Omeo couple, she's raised to follow the rules and emulate their marathon-length marriages by her counselor father.

Rules are made to be broken.

"Unmarried" to steamy and stormy, nonconformist Mamara, Ehra's rollicking ride begins with her partner's derelict brother missing from prison. Can they find him and undo his misdeeds before getting caught by cops and unraveling their rocky relationship?

Enter the Upperground

Love is a four-letter word.

Edgy romantic suspense thriller, Enter the Upperground continues where The Lie That Binds leaves off. Ehra stumbles on a secret society of unmatched people passing as Omeo, even as her second-class status stymies her every turn.

With her constant questions, "Uppergrounder" Hami challenges everything Ehra knows about the world and herself. Mamara's increasing volatility and an unexpected death thrusts Ehra into uncertainty. She is further devastated by Hami's dangerous declaration of love.

When Ehra receives a message from her father that could upend Omeo society, she faces her own bridges of Madison County between the highlife with Hami and domestic playacting with Mamara. With everything on the line, what future will she choose for herself and her adopted daughter?

Rise & Converge

The luck stops here.

A double dose of action and misadventure, Rise & Converge follows Ehra's transition into Jett as she starts a new life in the nation's capital, Cleveland. Her subversive policy proposal gets all the wrong attention as it threatens to upend unmatched inequities. And pressures of public life brought on by friendly fire strain her fragile new relationship to the breaking point.

Plus, one wrong slip of the tongue could undo everything and thrust her back into a life of groveling or worse.

Will she be able to hold her house together while she changes the world without revealing her identity?

Like This Book?

Please write a book review on Amazon, or Facebook. It really helps the author.

Share your favorite clip from this book on social media or recommend it to a friend.

For new release updates,
sign up for the author's newsletter:
SEChandlerBooks.com

Connect with S.E. Chandler online:
Facebook.com/SEChandlerBooks
SEChandlerBooks.com
Connect@SEChandlerBooks.com

For A Complete List of Books Visit:
SEChandlerBooks.com/Books

Acknowledgements

I first started this book in 2013 as part of National Novel Writing Month. I had just mainlined the first season of Orange is the New Black with my sister-in-law (holla, Summy!) over a working weekend in Kansas City. On the trip back home to Arkansas, these characters started having conversations and showing me scenes to write. I hadn't written fiction since undergrad and needed the support of a community alongside a major dose of inspiration to pull it off.

Although I wouldn't finish this story until years—and six seasons of OITNB—later, I'm grateful for the Nano community that got me through the first 50K words.

A special thanks to my brother, Barry Armstrong, who speaks Japanese (and several Asian languages), for helping me with the names and their meanings.

Finally, deepest gratitude to my mom, Elaine Gimblet, who read the book in 2013, asked me *repeatedly* to finish it, then read it all over again when I added the last chapter. I know you think everything I write is amazing (it isn't). And thanks for being convincing enough to make me believe in myself.

About the Author

S.E. Chandler

Subscribe for releases and updates at:
SEChandlerBooks.com

Email: Connect@SEChandlerBooks.com

Mother.
Mrs.
Writer.

First published as a poet on the wall of her elementary school in 1988, S.E. Chandler has spent decades dashing poems in private. After major life changes brought her to North Carolina, she cut her cable and wrote her first novel to celebrate finishing her MBA.

As part of her oxymoronic lifestyle, she is pursuing an MFA in Creative Writing at the Thomas Wolfe Center for Narrative at Lenoir-Rhyne University.

She and her wife live in Asheville where they enjoy momming two amazing babies, hiking in beautiful Western North Carolina and trying to stay married for the next 50 to 150 years.